Published through Create space by Soul Star Publishing a

division of Soul Star Multimedia

1621 Central Ave, Cheyenne, WY 82001

This is a work of fiction. Names, characters, places, and incidents either are the product of the author's imagination or are used fictitiously. Any resemblance to actual events, locales, organizations, or persons living or dead, is entirely coincidental and beyond the intent of either the author or the publisher.

Hampton Summit, the first book in the Castleton Series

Copyright ©2013 by Mike Dunbar

ISBN-13: 978-1482731620

ISBN-10: 1482731622

This book is dedicated to those members of Mrs. Santaniello's sixth grade reading class who graciously gave of their after school time to read and critique it for me.

Cover and chapter art by Sara Haley Santaniello

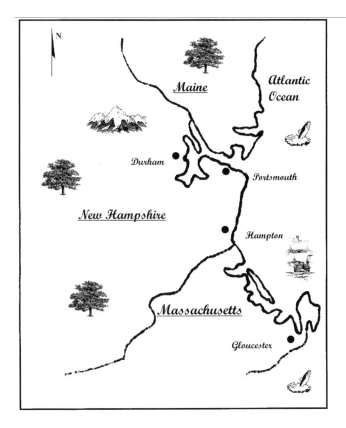

To Erica:
Happy reading

Chapter 1

Dr. Morley's Scheme

Seven generations from now…

Dr. Charles Newcomb was agitated as he strode purposefully up the MacDonald Center's walkway. As he passed the granite monument erected in front of the building and marking Dr. James MacDonald's grave, he slowed a moment to ponder. Was it possible that that Dr. MacDonald was going to die again, but this time in a different way? "Time travel does mess with your mind," he muttered, as he continued marching toward his destination.

The MacDonald Center is a large box-like brick building on the University of New Hampshire campus. As Dr. Newcomb entered, he passed a bronze plaque hanging on the wall. The plaque was as big as a kitchen table top and it dedicated the building to Dr. MacDonald. The metal plaque had hung there for so many decades it had turned the color of an old penny, everywhere but the lower right corner. It was a cadet custom to touch that spot for luck when they entered or exited. As a result, their fingers had polished that one corner so that it shone bright, like gold.

Dr. Newcomb continued down the building's main corridor with the same determined step. He was a short man, just a little over five feet tall. He was an older man, with wrinkles on his forehead and around his eyes. Much of his wavy hair was gray, and he had a bit of a pot belly. His bushy mustache was completely white. Dr. Newcomb wore a brown uniform that looked like a sweat suit. The color brown indicated that he was a teacher. However, he was also the Dean of Students.

As he strode down the hall, cadets and teachers, all the same height as the short dean, stepped aside. Normally, the others would have greeted Dr. Newcomb. Normally, he would have returned their greetings in a pleasant, friendly manner. Dr.

Newcomb usually wore an ever-present smile that invited such friendly exchanges. Not today. The others could tell by his serious expression he was preoccupied, and it would be inappropriate to distract him with mere pleasantries.

Dr. Newcomb was in too much of a hurry to wait for an elevator. Instead, he ran up the stairs to his third floor office, taking two steps at a time. He strode into his office in the same determined manner as he had entered the building. "Good Morning Dr. Newcomb" his assistant Mr. Takahashi said to the dean. "How was your trip to Washington?"

"It was very nice, Mr. Takahashi," Dr. Newcomb replied in a matter-of-fact tone. "Would you please contact Rabbi Cohen for me? Tell him I have to meet with him about an important matter. It is so urgent that he needs to clear his schedule. Tell him to plan on spending the rest of the day with me. Ask him to come here as soon as possible." With that Dr. Newcomb went into his private office and closed the door, leaving behind a stunned assistant. Dr. Newcomb was always friendly and courteous. What could have happened in Washington that would make him so abrupt, Mr. Takahashi wondered?

A while later, the assistant knocked on Dr. Newcomb's door and opened it a crack. "Rabbi Cohen has arrived. Shall I send him in?" the man asked tentatively.

"Yes, Mr. Takahashi. Please see him in. Then, please assure that we are not disturbed - under *any* circumstances."

Rabbi Jacob Cohen entered the office and shook his friend's hand. "How are you Charles?" the Rabbi asked. "Your message sounded ominous." In the closed office the two old friends dropped the formal tone they used with others. In private, they called each other by their first names.

Rabbi Jacob Cohen was small like Dr. Newcomb and wore a brown teacher uniform too. He was about the same age as the dean, but was more trim and wiry. He had dark bushy hair with some gray mixed in, and a full beard that he kept closely trimmed. He wore a yarmulke, a small round cap that covered the top of his head. The yarmulke sat on his bushy hair, held in place with a hair clip.

"Jacob, we have a problem bigger than anything you or I could imagine," Dr. Newcomb began. He gestured to a chair, inviting his friend to sit. It was obvious to the rabbi that this was going to take a while. "It's Roger, Jacob. Roger has had some sort of mental breakdown."

"You were called to Washington to meet with the Time Secretary because a teacher had a breakdown?" the Rabbi asked with surprise. A teacher's sanity was a concern for the Time Institute, but was hardly serious enough to involve higher ups.

"Yes and no," Dr. Newcomb continued. "The real reason for the trip was to be briefed on what Roger has done. Jacob, this is incredible. Roger has stolen a time craft and has gone back to Dr. James MacDonald's sequence. He plans to assassinate Dr. MacDonald."

Rabbi Cohen stared at his friend with his jaw open. A dozen questions raced through his mind. "Why?" the rabbi stammered. It was the only word he could manage.

"We will learn more this afternoon," Dr. Newcomb answered. "Roger has not been seen by our psychiatrists, but they have heard the story. They assume his brain tumor is back. The surgeons thought they had removed it all and he would return to teaching. This time, it seems to have caused a form of megalomania – a sense of being all important and all powerful. Roger plans nothing less than to become dictator of the whole world."

"How does killing Dr. MacDonald do that? Does Roger even know how to kill someone?" These were just some of the questions that swirled in Rabbi Cohen's confused mind. He shook his head in disbelief.

"I understand your reaction, Jacob," the dean said reassuringly. "I had the same response. Why? How? It doesn't make sense, but who knows what that tumor could be doing to his mind."

"Roger will set off a tsunami of Chaos that will sweep through history, from Dr. MacDonald's time to ours," Rabbi Cohen replied. "The damage will be on an unimaginable scale. No human being alive at that time - or born since - will escape harm. This time – our time – will never happen. The peace and prosperity we enjoy will disappear. Human history will go on being as violent and bloody as it was before the Hampton Summit."

"The Roswell Incident was the worst disaster we have ever had," Dr. Newcomb added. "That was a blip compared to this. Our Fixer teams fixed Roswell. An army of Fixers could never undo what Roger is planning. Our only option is to prevent it. We need to stop him. Let's have lunch, Jacob. At 1:00 we have a meeting in Room 307. We'll decide what to do once we're better informed."

The two teachers walked down the corridor from Dr. Newcomb's office to Room 307. This was a conference room with a long, oval table surrounded by chairs. The men took seats at the table where two other men in blue sweat suit-like uniforms were waiting for them. They were sitting on either side of a third man wearing a similar purple uniform. The two men in blue were full-sized adults, and they dwarfed the small man they were guarding. Still, the man in purple was so muscular he looked like he could give his guards a good fight. He was obviously much stronger than Dr. Newcomb or Rabbi Cohen.

Dr. Newcomb greeted the men in blue. "I want to thank you officers for bringing Mr. Gonzalez to meet with us. I think we are safe alone with him. Would you mind waiting outside while we talk?" The two security officers left the room, but glanced back with concern. They thought it too risky to leave their muscular prisoner alone with the two middle-aged teachers.

"Mr. Gonzalez," Dr. Newcomb began. "You are a member of our fleet's maintenance department. Correct?" The man in the purple uniform nodded. That explained the man's muscular build. Maintenance crews did heavy work, and they were all strong. "You maintain the cadet training craft?" The man nodded again. "Will you please tell us what transpired between you, your associates, and Dr. Roger Morley?"

"A couple of months ago Dr. Morley began to visit the hanger," Mr. Gonzalez began. "It's unusual to see a Researcher science observer at the hanger, but no one said anything about it. Dr. Morley talked with the maintenance crews, like he wanted to get to know us. During his first visits, it was just chit-chat. Then, he began to talk about things he had witnessed while studying the past. A lot of the maintenance people were uninterested. They paid him no mind when he visited. Others, including me, we listened to him. He was real smart and interesting. He told us about dictators from the past. It was fascinating to hear him describe all the marching, the uniforms, the flags, and the music.

"He said a lot of dictators had good ideas. Some of the other workers disagreed and stopped listening to him. Finally, it was just three of us who met with him when he visited."

"Besides you, who were the other two?" Rabbi Cohen asked.

"Lars Bryant and Collin Teller," the man answered. "We all do the same job; we take care of the training craft. We've worked together for a long time, but I don't know them very well. There's something about them that gives me the creeps. They're not very smart and I don't trust them. I only spent time with them because Dr. Morley was so fascinating."

"Continue your story," Dr. Newcomb asked the man.

"Like I said, Dr. Morley told us that dictators were not really bad people. In fact, they had lots of good ideas, ideas that would have helped everyone by making the world more efficient. However, other world leaders were jealous he said, and started wars with them. Even the strongest dictators couldn't take on the whole world. So, they lost. Dr. Morley said that was too bad, because the world would have been a better place if it had had been run by a dictator.

"Dr. Morley told us he had a plan that would correct history's mistakes. He said he had done a lot of research. He had learned everything a dictator needs to know. He said if he was dictator he wouldn't conquer just a country and its neighbors. He would take over the whole world. That way, there would be no one to start a war and stop him. He promised that if we would help him, he would make us part of his government. We would become powerful and important people."

"Very interesting," Rabbi Cohen responded. "What was the plan?"

"Dr. Morley wanted us to steal a time craft and take him into the past. Getting our hands on a time craft would be easy. We could leave on a test flight and just not come back. We'd pick up Dr. Morley and take him with us. No one would know where or when we went, so Fixer teams couldn't find us."

"What did Dr. Morley plan on doing in the past?" Dr. Newcomb asked the maintenance man.

"He planned on killing Dr. James MacDonald," Mr. Gonzalez answered, looking down in shame at his involvement.

So, this incredible story had been confirmed by someone who had been involved in it. The two teachers were shocked all over again. "How is Dr. Morley going to kill Dr. MacDonald?" Rabbi Cohen asked no one in particular. "We are peaceful. We don't have any weapons. How does he know how to kill someone? I don't have a clue how to do something as horrible as that."

Dr. Newcomb shook his head. He didn't have any answers for the rabbi. "There was plenty of killing in the past," he offered. "Most time crews have seen it. I assume Roger has."

"He didn't say how or when he would do it," Mr. Gonzalez explained. "He was keeping that a secret until we were ready. He did say that killing Dr. MacDonald would change so many sequences there would be Chaos everywhere. He would use it to take over as dictator. He said he had a plan how to do that, but he didn't tell it to us. We didn't care. For us, those were just details. We wanted those important jobs in his government. We wanted to help him make history right, the way it was supposed to have happened -the way it would have happened if Dr. MacDonald hadn't ruined everything with his discovery."

"I teach *History of Time Travel*," Rabbi Cohen said to Mr. Gonzalez. "I can tell you Dr. Morley is wrong. Dictators were not right, and they were not good. Dr. Morley has a brain tumor. He is a sick man."

"Yeah," Mr. Gonzalez answered in agreement. "I figured he was off his rocker. His plan made me queasy. It's not right to kill anyone. The stuff he told us sounded good at first, but I can't kill. Bryant and Teller, I believe they could kill someone, but not me. When Dr. Morley said someone had to stay behind and throw the Fixer teams off his trail, I agreed to do it. But it was just an excuse to get me out of this mess. As soon as they left, I went to the Security

Department. I can't believe what's happened to me since then. Everyone has made a fuss. I've even met with guys from the Department of Time in Washington."

"Do you have anything else to tell us?" Rabbi Cohen asked. Mr. Gonzalez shook his head. Dr. Newcomb called the two security men. "You understand why we have to detain you until we can stop Dr. Morley?" the rabbi asked. Mr. Gonzalez nodded his head in agreement. He stood and left Room 307 with the full-sized men in blue.

When the two teachers were alone again Dr. Newcomb rubbed his forehead like he had a headache. "What do you advise, Jacob?"

"Before we can stop Roger, we need to find him," the rabbi said, as if he were thinking out loud. "He can kill Dr. MacDonald at any time in the man's life and prevent his discovery. However, he does have this megalomania. The Hampton Summit is so famous and important it is the most likely place. I suggest we plant a Fixer team in Hampton just before the Summit to be our eyes and ears. We should also dispatch a Mapper team to map the sequences that lead up to the Summit. We need to identify all the important frames, in case we need to use them."

"Good idea," Dr. Newcomb said, agreeing with his friend. "I'll ask Kenneth and his team to take on the mission. They handled Roswell. However, I foresee some problems planting a Fixer team in that time. Fixers will be limited as to what they can do. They can't move around. They would be recognized as strangers immediately. We may speak the same language, but we know little about day-to-day life in the early 21st century. I'm afraid they'll make mistakes that will give them away. That would cause even more problems, and risk setting off even more Chaos."

"Here's an outlandish idea. I know we've never done this before," Rabbi Cohen said with hesitation in his voice, "But we've never had a situation like this before. Perhaps our Fixer team could enlist some help from that time period, from the people in town. Someone who lives in Hampton won't have the problem our Fixers face. They can come and go without raising any questions."

"That would be a big help," Dr. Newcomb mused. "But, it's an enormous risk. They would have to be extraordinary people, people we could trust to keep our work a secret."

"That's only part of the problem," Rabbi Cohen said. He grimaced as he realized how hard it would be to pull off his idea. "We don't know Roger's plan. Fixers learn all the procedures for fixing sequences when they are altered. However, this is different. To find Roger they need to think like Roger. Then, they have to be able to outwit him. We need people who are part detective and part gambler. They would have to be what we are not – innovative risk takers. Put all that together and it makes a tall order. I would tell Kenneth to plan on spending a long time in Hampton."

"A tall order with too many variables," Dr. Newcomb agreed. "We can't plan everything. I'm going to have to leave the details up to Kenneth and his team. Living in Hampton, they can search for the people we need. Once those people agree to help us, we need to train them. Without training in time travel ethics and procedures, they could cause Chaos. I don't see any other solution than to bring them to this time and put them through our cadet program. There's another problem to add to the list. These people have to have the aptitudes, and they cannot exceed our weight limitation."

"What a day this has been, Charles," Rabbi Cohen said, heaving a sigh and slumping in his chair. "First, we learn Roger plans to assassinate the most important man in history, to set off a tidal wave of

Chaos, and make himself dictator. We end up the day deciding to enlist people from the past to help us. We've spent our lives teaching cadets to avoid being discovered on missions. Now, we're sending a team to look for special people and to ask them to help us. And we are going to tell them all about time travel. *Oy-vay ist mir*," the exasperated rabbi muttered under his breath. He thought a moment longer and said, "The world has been turned upside down, Charles. Everything is topsy-turvy and I don't like it. It is too risky. I prefer our nice safe procedures."

Chapter 2
The Hampton Summit

Eight years from now…

Dr. James A. MacDonald's claw-like left hand pushed the joy stick on his electric wheelchair, starting his chair gently forward. Its small fat tires rolled across the ballroom floor. When he was a young man, an incurable illness had attacked Dr. MacDonald's muscles and left his legs limp and useless. As he grew older, his ancient enemy continued its persistent assault on his body. The illness was now attacking his arms and weakening them. It had already caused his fingers to curl up like a bird's foot.

The band that was providing music before the summit was wrapping up its last number. As the song came to an end, the singer jumped in the air. This was a signal to the others. As his feet reached the floor, the band stopped on cue. As Dr. MacDonald rolled past he nodded to the singer/guitar player and mouthed, "Thank you."

The band was made up of five young men and a young woman. On the bass drum there was a picture of a mermaid with her hands to her mouth. She was singing. Although they were a rock band, the musicians all wore jackets and ties. The singer and lead guitar player wore a captain's hat. He hung his guitar from his shoulder with a fuzzy, hot pink strap.

Dr. MacDonald rolled slowly up the long, low ramp to the stage where he was to speak. When he reached the table set up for him he turned his chair to face the audience. The chair's electric motor made a loud click each time he changed directions.

Dr. MacDonald's legs and hands might not work any longer, but his mind still did. It was a great mind. The biology professor from the University of New Hampshire was recognized as one of the world's leading scientists. In fact, he had recently made an astounding discovery, perhaps the greatest scientific advance of all time. He was here today to give that discovery to the world.

Dr. MacDonald scanned the sea of faces sitting in front of him. He had invited all these people to the little seaside town of Hampton, New Hampshire. They had gathered in the ballroom at Oakwood, right across from the beach. If he turned and looked out the ballroom's front windows Dr. MacDonald would see the Atlantic Ocean. It was a fitting place for this summit, right next to the sea. In two harvests the world would be flooded by an ocean of food. In another few years it would be awash in a tide of cheap, clean bio-fuel.

The ballroom was packed with people. Scientists and researchers attended from important universities around the world. Most countries had sent government officials. Many of the people attending the summit wore their national dress, creating a colorful and diverse audience.

A team of Dr. MacDonald's students sat on the stage behind him. A row of hotel workers stood against the walls. Some were the wait staff and were going to serve champagne at the end of the summit.

The others had snuck away from their posts and into the ballroom to witness history.

FBI agents and police officers were mixed with the hotel workers, but the real security was outside. The United States government was worried about a terrorist attack. What a great target, so many important people from all over the world, gathered together in one place. To prevent an attack, marksmen on the hotel roof scanned the area around the building with binoculars. They examined every car and truck, checking out anything that could carry a weapon or a bomb. So far, so good. There had been no problems.

Dr. MacDonald looked out over the audience and raised his arms as high as he could. It was not very high. His muscles were so weak he could barely get his hands level with his shoulders. He had raised his arms to ask the people who were standing to sit, and to ask people who were talking to stop.

"Ladies and Gentlemen," he began. This was a signal to the hotel workers. He paused while they closed the ballroom doors. The Hampton Summit was finally underway. "Ladies and Gentlemen, the reason for you being here today has been kept secret. You came because you had faith in my reputation. Thank you for your trust. You will find it was well placed.

"Several years ago, I was working on a new strain of wheat when I discovered an unknown gene in cereal and grain plants. The gene is not normally active, which means in nature it is turned off. I found a way to turn it on. Ladies and Gentlemen, this gene controls plant growth. In the off position, cereals and grains grow at the rate they normally do. If the gene is turned on, plants grow fast and in huge amounts. The gene makes cereals and grains so strong that they are not harmed by drought or cold.

"Ladies and Gentlemen, I am giving you my discovery to take home with you. You are about to end hunger. Soon, there will be more food than people can eat. It will become so cheap the poor can buy all they want. If they can't buy it, they can grow their own. All they need is dirt. In two years, a single seed will create a field of food. There will never be another famine."

The audience was confused and stared at Dr. MacDonald with disbelief. They were not sure what to think. Some guessed Dr. MacDonald was trying to start his speech with a joke. If so, he was not doing it very well. This joke was not funny. Others suspected a hoax. It had happened before. Other scientists had made false claims about amazing discoveries. Some in the audience even wondered if Dr. MacDonald had gone crazy. Perhaps his illness was now attacking his mind.

"There is an energy shortage. It too is going to end," the scientist continued. "Left over plants can be turned into bio-fuels, clean alternatives for gasoline and heating oil. Energy will become cheap and there will be lots of it - everywhere."

The audience was becoming unhappy with these outrageous statements. A buzz rose from the crowd. People had stopped paying attention to him and were talking with their neighbors about his crazy claim. Some even stood up to walk out. "I see you do not believe me," he said into the microphone, raising his voice to speak over the noise. "I have grown some of these plants. I have some seeds with me. They are in this box on the table." That worked. The audience was curious and grew quiet. People who had stood up to leave sat back in their chairs.

"This discovery is so important I will not let anyone profit from it," Dr. MacDonald told his audience. "I will give it to the whole world so no one can own it and no one can control it. There is a wireless network in this room. You were all asked to bring a laptop or a tablet, so we are connected. I am going to send the process from my laptop to yours. It will happen with a push of a button and at the speed of light. Once that occurs, my discovery will belong to the world."

One of Dr. MacDonald's students stood up and walked to his laptop to help him. She opened a new email message and attached a file named *abundance*. She stepped back so Dr. MacDonald could use the keyboard.

"Everyone. Please open your email." He waited as hundreds of people did as he asked. This time, the noise from the audience was the clicking of computer keys. Dr. MacDonald could not resist adding a bit of drama to the moment. He extended the first finger of his right hand as much as he could. It was not very straight; his hands were too weak. He held his bent finger upward so everyone could see it. Everyone watched, waiting for his finger to move downward and touch his keyboard. When that happened, he would send the document.

Dr. MacDonald slowly lowered his finger. His disabled hand shook as it made its way to the keyboard. **"Pop! Pop! Pop!"** A series of staccato sounds broke out around the room. The audience gasped. **"Pop! Pop! Pop!"** Some delegates knew that noise. It was small caliber pistols, the weapons favored by assassins. They dove for the floor. **"Pop! Pop! Pop!"** Police officers and FBI agents unsnapped their holsters and pulled out their guns. The students on stage jumped to their feet as they watched their teacher slump over his wheelchair's right arm rest. They saw his hand slide away from the computer without touching the keyboard. One of the students screamed, "He's been hit! He's been hit!"

Chapter 3
The Sirens

The present.....

It was the last day of summer vacation. Twelve-year old Mike Castleton rode in the passenger's seat of his mother's van as she drove down a peaceful residential street in Hampton, New Hampshire. Mike had two features that people noticed right away. First, were his eyes. They were big and they were deep blue, with long eyelashes and thick eyebrows. His mother's friends always admired them.

They said they were jealous and that eyes that beautiful were wasted on a boy. Second, Mike's face was covered with freckles. They were not the big dark kind. They were small, light dots, but they were sprinkled all over his face like they had been put there with a pepper shaker.

Mike had a round head and his ears stuck out just a bit more than he liked. To tease him, his father called him Charlie Brown. His mother told him not to worry. His face would get longer as he aged and he would grow into his ears. Mike had gained a few inches in the past year, but was disappointed that his head was still shaped like a soccer ball.

Mike's hair was dark brown and straight. He had fair skin. He smiled a lot and had a quick sense of humor. His off-hand comments always made his friends laugh. He did have an odd habit. When Mike was thinking he would speak his thoughts out loud.

Mrs. Castleton turned into the driveway of a small ranch-style house. Two boys dressed in shorts and tee shirts were standing in front of the garage door. Anyone could see they were brothers, they looked so much alike. The brothers were playing street hockey. They had tied a plastic pail on top of a garbage can to use as a target. It was on its side with the open end facing the boys. The older brother dropped a puck onto the driveway and slapped the small black disk into the bucket.

"Hi Nick," Mike called as he waved out the window to his friend Nick Pope. Nick was shorter than Mike, and he was a lot thinner. In fact, Nick was skinny. Nick's father was a tall man, so everyone knew that someday Nick was going to grow a lot. For now, he was small for his age.

Nick had deep brown eyes and olive-colored skin. Mike would burn in the sun, while Nick would get a good tan. Nick's hair was the same color as Mike's, but it never looked combed. It was a wild mop with a mind of its own.

Nick was shy and he spoke quietly. He never joked and he didn't smile a lot. He always looked worried. He wasn't worried. He just looked that way.

Mike opened the car door and stepped out. "Wanna try?" Nick asked, offering Mike his hockey stick.

"I'm not sure I know what end to hold," Mike joked. It was his way of saying he didn't know a lot about hockey.

"Take a try," Nick replied as he dropped a puck in front of Mike. Mike hit it, trying to imitate what he had seen Nick do. The puck slammed into the garage wall, leaving a dark scuff mark.

"I may not be cut out for hockey," said Mike sheepishly, giving the stick back to Nick.

Nick showed off his skill for his friend. He put four pucks in his pocket and held one in his hand. He dropped the puck and swung the stick. The puck flew into the air and slammed into the bucket like a bullet. Two, three, four, five. One after another the pucks from Nick's pocket banged into the bucket.

Mike watched with admiration. "You're a goalie aren't you, Nick?" he asked.

"Yeah," Nick answered with his usual serious expression. "I want to be a wingman, but my coach says I'm not big enough."

Nick went into the house to put away his hockey stick and came back out carrying a guitar case. Mrs. Pope stood in the door and waved. "I'll bring Nick back before supper," Mrs. Castleton called to Mrs. Pope.

Mrs. Castleton's van drove up the long driveway to the Castleton house. The house was a small cottage set far back from the road and surrounded by forest. In front of the house was a colorful carpet of carefully arranged flowers and plants. Mike and Nick piled out of the car and went inside, headed upstairs for Mike's bedroom. They had not been there long when a black car drove down the drive. It stopped at the house and a third boy, Patrick Weaver stepped out.

Mrs. Castleton walked to the car to chat with Patrick's father. "They're up in Michael's room, dear," Mrs. Castleton said to Patrick. "Go ahead up."

The boys heard Patrick on the stairs and Mike called down to him, "Up here." Once in the room, Patrick threw himself backward onto Mike's bed. Patrick had blue eyes and freckles too. His eyes were not as blue as Mike's and his freckles were limited to his nose. Patrick's skin was fair like Mike's, but his hair was sandy color, lighter than either of his friends.

Patrick was short like Nick, but he wasn't skinny. He wasn't fat either. He was just wide and strong. Patrick was the heaviest and strongest of the three. Patrick was not funny like Mike, but he was not shy like Nick. Patrick was matter-of-fact and did not waste words. He spoke like a kid who had a job to do and was determined to do it.

"How you guys been?" Patrick asked his friends. The boys had not been all together since the last day of school in June when they had completed the fifth grade at Atlantic Academy. This was the last day of summer vacation and tomorrow they would begin the sixth grade.

"How was Ti Kwon Do camp?" asked Nick.

"It was awesome," replied Patrick happy to talk about his favorite activity. "I'll have no trouble making black belt now. I learned some really great stuff."

"Like what?" Mike asked.

"The best thing was how to disarm someone. It's a really cool move," said Patrick. He stood up and told Mike, "Act like you've pulled a gun on me."

Mike stepped in front of Patrick and pointed his finger like a gun. "Don't move or I'll shoot," he said, pretending to be a bad guy.

Patrick moved in slow motion so as to not hurt his friend. His left arm came up and pushed Mike's right hand aside. He held on to Mike's wrist as he turned away from Mike and slipped under his friend's arm. Patrick came up behind Mike pinning his arm behind his back.

"Wow," said Mike. Patrick had moved so smoothly he had caught him by surprise. Even though the whole maneuver was done in slow motion Mike felt completely helpless as Patrick wound his way behind him.

"That's awesome," Nick agreed.

"What did you guys do this summer?" asked Patrick.

"Nick went to hockey camp," Mike answered. "You should see him hit a puck."

"I restored an antique sports car with my grandfather too," Nick added. "We worked in his garage almost every day. When we finished he let me drive it."

"On the street?" asked Patrick in amazement.

"No, just in the parking lot," replied Nick. The other two were still impressed. Nick had to be the first kid in Atlantic Academy's sixth grade to drive a car.

"It's not easy," Nick said. "The car has a standard transmission. You have to shift gears as you go faster." Patrick and Mike sat on the bed and admired their friend.

"I learned a new type of math," said Patrick, breaking the silence. Mike and Nick looked at him blankly. They knew Patrick was good at math, but how he could enjoy it? How could he find math fun? "It's called Singapore Math," explained Patrick. "It's how kids learn math in Asia. The Singapore method makes a lot more sense, and you learn a whole lot more. I'm doing problems even the eighth graders don't do. In fact, I'm gonna be in the morning algebra class?"

"Huh?" asked Nick.

"The morning algebra class," Patrick repeated. "Mrs. Sampson the math teacher told my father she thought I could do it and would recommend me to Miss Watson. It's a class for all the best math students in the eighth grade. I'm not happy I have to be with those older kids. I know they'll give me a hard time, especially if I'm better than they are."

Nick and Mike stared at Patrick. They had no idea this math class even existed. Patrick could tell by their looks they didn't understand. "Okay," he said slowly. "There's this special class. It meets one hour before school. It's for eighth graders who are good at math. If they pass that class, they can go into honors math in high school. I'll be the only sixth grader in it."

There it was. Patrick would have to go to school an hour earlier. He would be in a class full of eighth graders and he was going to do really hard math. To top it off, he was excited. Mike and Nick could not get their heads around it. Patrick again broke the silence. "How was Space Camp?" he asked Mike.

"It was awesome," replied Mike, happy to change the subject from math.

"Do anything different than last time?" asked Nick.

"Oh yeah," Mike answered. "Last time was a parent/child weekend. My dad and I went together and it was for only three days. This time the camp was a whole week, and it was just for kids. Some were my age, but most were older.

"We did a simulated shuttle mission. I scuba dived in this huge tank to learn what weightlessness feels like. You know, in space you don't have any place to put your feet. You try to turn a wrench, but all you do is turn your body.

"We've got a lot of stuff to learn if we're gonna go to Mars. Working in space is hard. The food is something else. It's all in these foil packs, and you don't want to know about the toilets," Mike rambled in his enthusiasm. He went to his closet and came out carrying a stack of notebooks. "I did the research this summer too," he said. "I studied all sorts of stuff, like astronomy, Mars, spacecraft, rocket engines."

Nick and Patrick looked at the pile. "Whoa Mike. That's like a whole year of homework," said Nick.

"It's all stuff we have to know," Mike replied. "I got lots more work to do."

"Boys," Mike's mother called up the stairs. "Lunch." The boys went down to find peanut butter and jelly sandwiches, chocolate chip cookies, and glasses of milk waiting for them on the kitchen table.

"Well, Patrick," asked Mrs. Castleton "Did you have a good summer?"

"Yes, 'Mam," replied Patrick.

"Are you two ready to go back to school?" she asked Nick and Patrick. The two boys groaned. They did not want summer vacation to end.

"Well, just think, you'll be in the sixth grade," Mrs. Castleton said with a smile. "You're junior high schoolers and you're officially upper classman at Atlantic Academy. You get to wear a white shirt and tie this year."

"That means we'll get pushed around by eighth graders, Mom," protested Mike. "They love to give sixth graders a hard time. They ignore you when you're in the fifth grade, but sixth grade is really tough."

"Well, you have nothing to worry about," Mrs. Castleton added reassuringly. "You three are a team and you can always count on each other."

Patrick, Nick, and Mike had been friends since pre-school. In the second grade they discovered they all wanted to be astronauts. They decided they would be the first people to land on Mars. To practice for their careers in space they explored the woods around

Mike's house, pretending they were astronauts in a forest on an alien planet.

When the boys finished their sandwiches and cookies Mike asked, "Mom, can we be excused? I want to play Nick and Patrick a song I wrote."

"Certainly son," replied his mother. "Remember; keep the power down on your amplifier. You don't want to hurt Menlo's ears. Dogs have better hearing than humans. Loud music is painful for them."

The inventor Thomas Edison was one of Mike's heroes, and Edison's laboratory was in Menlo Park, New Jersey. That's where his dog got his name. Menlo was a foxhound. He was a handsome dog, covered with large brown and white patches. However, everyone first noticed his tail. The half attached to him was black. The second half - all the way to the tip - was pure white. Menlo's tail was J shaped. Most of the time it stuck out straight from his rump, and curled upward, but when the dog got excited or was on alert, his tail stood erect and curled over his back. No matter what position it was in, his tail was always wagging.

"Okay," Mike answered his mother. "Come on guys," he said to the others, leading them down to the cellar where he kept his musical instruments. Menlo went with the boys and plopped down near the drums to sleep. He kept one eye half open so he would know if the boys got up to leave.

"Listen to this, Nick," Mike said to his friend. He picked up a black and white electric guitar with a fuzzy pink shoulder strap and turned on the amp. He tuned the guitar by plucking the strings while turning the tuning pegs with his other hand. Then, he put a captain's hat on his head. "This is my trademark hat. It's part of my identity as a rocker," he said.

Mike played some sad blues music he had written. Nick and Patrick were only twelve years old and had never been really sad in their lives. That's why this music surprised them. It created strange feelings in them, feelings that turned into sad thoughts. Patrick thought about a man in love, but his woman had left him. Nick thought about someone losing a dog.

"Did you really write that?" Nick asked when Mike finished.

"Yeah," answered Mike. "I really did. I was down here one day a while ago playing some chords and it came to me. I don't know where it came from, it just sort of got into my head." Usually, Nick and Patrick teased Mike when he said weird things like that. But they had just heard the music and they felt the feelings it created in them. Mike continued, "Music just comes into my head. Sometimes it happens when I'm playing the guitar. I even wake up sometimes and remember some new music, like I had heard it in a dream. I lay awake and I go over and over it in my head so I'll remember it. The next day, I play the music on my guitar and record it on my laptop."

Nick took out his guitar. It was a bass, a type of guitar that only plays deep, low notes. Nick's bass was a bit longer than Mike's guitar and had four strings, instead of six. "Play it again," Nick told Mike. Mike began the music and Nick joined in.

"Wow," said Patrick when the two were done. "That was really good! When did you two guys start playing together?"

"After school got out," Mike answered. "You'd gone off to camp. We got together a couple of times to jam. We found we play real well together. We decided we're gonna start a band. We already picked out the name – the Sirens. The Sirens were a type of Mermaid. Their singing hypnotized sailors so they wrecked their boats on the rocks and drowned."

"I wish I could play like that," said Patrick.

"We do need a drummer," Mike responded with enthusiasm. "I could teach you if you wanted to learn." Patrick agreed. Mike sat his friend down at his drum set and explained the different drums. He showed Patrick how to keep a beat. "You'll catch on fast," he told Patrick. "I have a DVD on how to play the drums. Take it home. Take a pair of my drum sticks too. You can practice on anything hard, like a book.

"If we're gonna be a band, we need to practice every week," Mike added. "We can do it here in my cellar." The boys jammed the rest of the afternoon and Patrick got pretty good as a drummer.

At five o'clock Mrs. Castleton called down to the boys. "Michael, it's almost five. Patrick, your father will be here soon. Nick, I promised to bring you home before supper." The boys came upstairs, followed by Menlo.

Soon, Patrick's father drove down the long driveway and Patrick ran out to meet him. As the car drove away Patrick leaned out the open window and waved goodbye to his friends.

"See you at school tomorrow," Mike called.

Chapter 4
Double A

It was eight o'clock on the first day of school at Atlantic Academy, dubbed *Double A* by the students. The parking lot was a busy place. A long line of cars stretched around the school. One at a time, the cars pulled up to the front of the building and dropped off children who got into line with their class. The kids were weighed down with full back packs. Double A was a private school and well-known for its high academic standards. That meant lots of homework, every night and weekends too.

Lines of students, divided by grade, formed in front of the school and waited. At 8:10 a teacher blew a whistle, the signal to start into the building. One at a time the lines moved forward, led by their teachers. The shorter lines joined end-to-end and became one long line. From a distance the students looked like an army on the march. When the long line reached the building the army divided in two columns. The lower grades walked to the rear door and went in there. The upper grades went in through the front door. They took the stairs to the second floor, where their classrooms were.

Like an army, the students all wore uniforms. This made it easy to tell the junior high school kids from the primary school, even at a distance. Junior high boys wore white shirts and Atlantic Academy ties, striped gray and blue. They had black pants and black shoes. The girls wore white blouses and gray pleated skirts or gray slacks.

Mike arrived at the sixth grade line. He found Nick and stood with him. As his class moved to join the long line, Mike looked around. "No Patrick," he said to Nick with concern in his voice. Nick reminded Mike that Patrick's morning math class had started an hour ago.

The line of sixth graders entered the school's front door and immediately turned to climb the stairs. There, at the bottom of the stairs stood the school principal, Miss Watson. Miss Watson was a tiny woman, only about five feet tall. She had gray hair but her skin was smooth, with no wrinkles or age lines. Her hair style, her eye glasses, and her clothes were all ten years out of date. When he spotted the principal Mike thought to himself that Miss Watson still looked the same as she did when he started in the Atlantic Academy pre-school, all those years ago.

Miss Watson was serious and strict. Her face was emotionless. She did not frown, but she did not smile either. Mostly, she watched in an intense manner that made kids feel she was seeing inside them. Way back in pre-school Patrick, Nick, and Mike had learned to fear Miss Watson. No one told them they should fear her, or why. Like all the other kids at Double A, they just knew they should.

Expressionless, Miss Watson examined the sixth grade class as it paraded by. Most kids looked away, like they even feared passing close to her. A few brave ones summoned enough courage to greet their small principal. "Good morning, Miss Watson," Mike said nervously.

"Good morning, Mr. Castleton," Miss Watson replied without any warmth or emotion. "Welcome to the sixth grade." Mike was surprised. Teachers had always called him by his first name - Mike. He recalled the instructions Miss Watson had given the fifth grade last June as school ended. "Middle school students are called Mister or Miss," she had told them. "This is a sign of respect. You are becoming young adults. Teachers will speak to you as young adults and you will be treated as young adults," she said. "For your part, we expect you to speak and act like polite young adults. We expect this *all the time*."

Miss Watson had another rule that applied to the entire school, not just the junior high. "You will not use slang or street talk. You will always speak in correct English." She was really strict about this rule and as a result, kids at Double A were polite and well-spoken.

Mike and Nick felt better when they got to the landing where they could no longer see Miss Watson, and where she could no longer see them. They went to their lockers and then to their homeroom. Their homeroom teacher was standing next to the door greeting the students. Mike and Nick went in and found Patrick already at his desk. They sat next to him.

Math was Patrick's best subject and he loved the morning math class. Nick liked to work with his hands, so computer was his preferred class. The teacher relied on Nick to fix things. As a result, he usually worked under a desk, not at one.

Mike loved science, but that was not his favorite class. He liked his Music class best, and he liked his music teacher, Mr. Newcomb. The teacher's first name was Charles. Of course, Mike only called him Mr. Newcomb, or Sir.

Mike had great talks with his teacher. He told Mr. Newcomb that when he wrote music he heard it in his head and in his heart. His music was different from any music he knew of. "Mr. Castleton," asked Mr. Newcomb. "Do you know what Chamber Music is?"

"No," Mike answered.

"Chamber Music was written for small groups of people. It was played in a room, not an auditorium. That's what the word chamber means – a room. Some Chamber Music was really audacious. Do you know what that word means? Audacious? It means daring. Audacious people take risks. They try new things. I have some Chamber Music CDs I will lend you. Listen to them. They may give you some ideas."

Even though the boys were all in the sixth grade, they only had one class together, Social Studies with Mr. Kenneth Smith. Mr. Smith was a short black man, small like Miss Watson. Some of the sixth graders were already as tall as he was. The teacher was small, but he was trim and fit, like he worked out. Mr. Smith's skin was deep brown, the rich color of chocolate. He was bald, except for a ring of short gray hair. The top of his head was so shiny, light reflected off it. Mr. Smith had a thin mustache that he smoothed regularly with the tip of his index finger. The whiskers were so short they did not need smoothing; he stroked them as a nervous habit.

Everyone said Mr. Smith was weird, and everyone was right. The teacher was very odd. Yeah, he knew all about Social Studies, but when it came to everyday things, he was brain dead. He had never heard of most television shows. He didn't know there were different makes of cars. He didn't even know who the Red Sox were. "It's like he's from another planet," Mike said one day at lunch. "He's so smart, but he's so dumb about other stuff. Where's he been all his life?"

The first day of class, Mr. Smith assigned Nick, Mike, and Patrick desks in the front row. Teachers sat problem students up front where they could keep an eye on them. The boys never caused trouble, so they wondered why Mr. Smith put them there.

One day after Social Studies class Patrick said, "Smith gives me the creeps. Do you get the feeling he's watching us? Sometimes I feel like we're under a microscope. He will say something, and then he watches us. Do you notice? Another kid will say something, and he asks us what *we* think? He's like Miss Watson in math."

"What do you mean?" Mike asked with surprise.

"Miss Watson comes into math class sometimes pretending she's there to observe the teacher. I get the feeling she's watching just me. It's weird. I can't explain it. I just feel the same way I do about Mr. Smith."

"Strange," said Mike thinking aloud.

"Now, what do *you* mean?" Patrick asked.

"The same thing happens in science class," Mike answered. "Miss Watson comes in with a clipboard like she's there to check out the teacher and the class. When I answer a question, she takes notes. She doesn't do it with the other kids, just me. Sometimes, she'll even ask me a question, like she's the teacher."

"I know what you mean," added Nick with his usual worried expression. "Only it happens to me in computer class. She comes in and sits down in the lab. When I'm fixing something she'll come over and watch. Then, she'll ask me stuff like, how did I know how to fix that? What do I think when I'm working? I don't know the answers. I don't know how I know stuff. I just do. I can see how things go together. I can see how parts work. I don't know what I'm thinking. I'm thinking I gotta fix this thing. What does she mean, what am I thinking? Or, how am I thinking? It's too weird for me."

"I don't like Miss Watson watching me," said Mike. "I don't want her to know I exist. I wish I was invisible so she couldn't see me. I just want to get outta Double A without being sent to her office."

"She never paid any attention to us before," Patrick said. "What did we do this year?"

Miss Watson and Mr. Smith made the boys nervous. Mrs. Martin, a second grade teacher made them miserable. Mrs. Martin was a short, heavy woman who always wore loose dresses with big, flower prints. She tinted her hair in her bathroom sink, and the result was a weird color that was supposed to be red, but was more orange. Mrs. Martin had a sour face, accentuated by her eye glasses. They were the old fashioned kind, the type with tear drop-shaped lenses and heavy, bright plastic frames. Mrs. Martin never smiled, and she yelled a lot. The boys remembered how relieved they were in the second grade when they were placed in Miss Brown's class, rather than Mrs. Martin's.

Somewhere along the line, they must have crossed Mrs. Martin, although they didn't know how. There was no denying the dislike she had for them. She made it her job to pick on them whenever possible. After lunch and recess she waited outside her classroom with her arms crossed and a frown on her face. When the boys walked by she always had some threat. "That hair needs to be combed, Mr. Pope. Come by my room. I'll take care of it for you." Or, "Those shoes are scuffed Mr. Weaver. Get them shined or I'll give you a detention." Or, "Your tie is too loose, Mr. Castleton. Tighten it. You won't like it if I tighten it. You won't be able to breathe."

This was their world. After eight years at, Atlantic Academy Mike, Nick, and Patrick knew the playing field and all the players. Except for Mrs. Martin and the recent attention they were getting from Miss Watson and Mr. Smith, their lives at Double A were pretty good. They were three normal, happy kids having a good year. That was about to change.

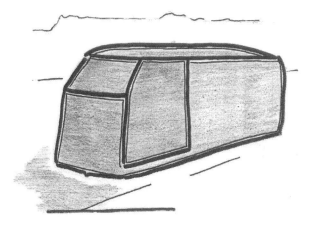

Chapter 5
The Close Encounter

One day in November Mike hurried into homeroom and sat beside Nick and Patrick. His expression told his friends he had something exciting. "I've got some great news," he said. "I was in the woods behind my house yesterday after school. You know that huge oak tree on the edge of the pond? The beavers dropped it so it fell right across, all the way to the other side. They made us a bridge."

This was good news, and it excited Patrick and Nick just as much as Mike. They knew the pond well. It was where they played when pretending to be an astronaut team sent down to explore a new planet. A stream flowed into one end of the pond and out the other. So, there was no way around it. They could only play in the woods on one side. They could see the woods on the other side, but they couldn't get there to explore. This would be like a real mission to an undiscovered country.

"Meet at my house at 10:00 Saturday morning," Mike told his friends. "Don't forget your gear."

That Saturday, Patrick, Nick, and Mike assembled in the Castleton kitchen, each boy wearing a matching back pack. "Let's check the gear," Patrick advised. "Remember, once we beam down we can't come back if we forgot something.

"Communicators," he said. He held up his walkie-talkie to show he had his.

"Check," Nick and Mike responded.

"Ray guns."

"Check."

"Binoculars."

"Check."

"Canteens."

"Check."

"Pencil and pad."

"Check."

"Specimen containers."

"Check."

"Chow."

"Check," said Mrs. Castleton. She had made lunch for the boys. She gave each one a peanut butter and jelly sandwich, wrapped in a sandwich bag. Next, she gave each of them three chocolate chip cookies, also in bags. Finally, she gave each one a juice box.

"Remember to always leave a new planet the way you found it. Carry in. Carry out. No litter," she teased.

"Oh, Mom," Mike groaned.

Patrick led the way to the pond, but the other two didn't need to be guided. They had gone this way so many times they knew every step along the path. At the pond they spotted the huge oak stretched across from one bank to the other. The boys stopped a minute to examine the beavers' work. The animals' powerful teeth had sliced thick bites of wood from the living tree and the fresh chips littered the ground around the stump.

The tree created a perfect bridge. Patrick jumped up on the trunk, followed by the other two. The team made its way across without anyone getting his feet wet. On the other side Patrick, Nick, and Mike paused to look at the wall of trees in front of them. It was November, so the leaves had all fallen off. Everything was brown, instead of green. "Well, here we are. We're on a newly discovered planet," Patrick announced. "There are trees on this planet, so there are probably higher life forms. Be on the lookout. If we meet intelligent life, we are first contact. Remember our directive. We observe, but we don't change anything. Set your weapons on stun, for defense only.

"Standard procedure," Patrick said. "Split up and form a line. I'll take the middle. Mike, you'll be on my left. Nick, you're on the right. Maintain communicator contact at all times." The three boys spread out, and on Patrick's command they advanced straight ahead into the woods until they could no longer see each other.

Nick called on his walkie-talkie, "I'm observing strange plant life growing on the trees. It's green, soft, and hairy. I'm taking samples."

"There are odd rock formations," Mike reported. "I think this planet is still volcanically active. The rocks look geologically recent. I'll take samples to study in the lab."

"I see a small animal in a tree," said Nick. "It looks like a mammal. It's gray and has a bushy tail. I'm writing a description and drawing a picture."

"There are feathered flying creatures," Mike added. "I just scared two. They took off from a bush in front of me. They were too fast for me to see details." The boys moved on, Nick and Mike radioing regular reports.

Looking ahead through the tops of the trees, Patrick could see a patch of sky. The sky told him he was coming to an open space. "I have found a clearing," he whispered into his radio. "I am using caution. It may be a village for intelligent life. Join me on my coordinates. Standard procedure. Maintain communicator silence."

Nick and Mike each joined up with Patrick at the same time. Mike came in on his left, and Nick on the right. Patrick was crouched behind a tree staring into the clearing, still as a stone. Mike and Nick hunched over and moved slowly and silently in toward Patrick. They crouched behind trees too, and looked ahead into the clearing to see what Patrick had found.

Mike and Nick knew right away that Patrick wasn't pretending, or playing. They knew, because they each saw what had frozen their friend in position.

The same fear seized them and froze them in place. Each boy wanted to run away, but their bodies wouldn't work. All they could do was stare. They couldn't even blink.

There were two objects in the clearing that resembled Volkswagen busses. Those are the kind of busses the Hippies used to drive. They were shaped like a big loaf of bread on wheels. Only these box-shaped objects didn't have any wheels or windows, and they weren't covered in flowers and peace signs. They were a solid silvery color. The objects had to be some form of craft, because they both had open doors. Six small figures stood between the boxy craft. The figures were all shaped like humans – head, arms, legs - but three were all gray, and three were all green. All six had large, black oval eyes.

Even though the frightened boys could not see any mouths, the figures seemed to be communicating. They moved their hands the way people do when they talk. The figures stood between the objects for about 10 minutes. Once, one of them went into a craft and came back out. At last, the gray ones got into one craft, while the three greens got into the other. The doors closed and instantly, the two objects disappeared.

The terrified boys remained crouched behind their trees and continued to stare into the clearing. Each was cold and shaking, and their mouths were dry. Finally, Patrick stood up and began to move slowly forward. Mike and Nick followed behind him, just as cautiously.

The three boys walked around the clearing and examined it. Other than freshly turned leaves where the figures had stood, there was no sign anything had just happened.

"Did you guys see that?" Patrick finally asked.

"Yeah," Nick and Mike answered.

"What was it?" Patrick continued. "Were those UFOs?"

"They had to be," Mike replied. "I've seen drawings of aliens on television and in books. They looked just that."

"Did we just have a close encounter?" Nick added, like he didn't believe what he had seen.

Patrick's body began to react to the scare. He sat down in the clearing and bent his knees toward his chest. He put his arms around his legs and shook in fear. Mike and Nick put their arms around their chests like they were trying to hug themselves. They shook too. Mike rocked slowly back and forth.

More time went by without anyone speaking. Finally, Nick asked, "What are we gonna do? Who can we tell?"

"I want to tell my Dad," Mike answered. "Maybe he'll know what to do."

"Will he believe us?" asked Patrick.

"I hope so," Mike replied. Then, he kicked some dead leaves. "I have my cell phone with me. If I wasn't so scared I could've taken some video. Then, we'd have proof. Geez!" he said, angry at himself.

The boys fell silent again. Patrick stood up and led his friends back to the tree bridge and across the pond. From there, they walked along the path to the Castleton house. Mike and his friends went into the family room where Mike's father sat reading a book. "Dad?" Mike asked. His father put the book down and looked at his son. "Dad, we just saw two UFOs and some aliens. They were in the woods on the other side of the pond."

"That's great, son," his father replied with a smile. "I'm glad you boys had a good time."

"No, really, Dad. We saw aliens."

"Well, as long as they're friendly, I guess we have nothing to worry about," his father responded as he returned to his reading.

The boys went to the cellar where they held their band practices. "He didn't believe us," said Nick.

"He didn't even take us seriously," Mike added. "He thought we were still playing."

"Let's face it," Patrick advised his friends. "We can't tell anyone, 'cause no one's gonna believe us. We can't tell any adults. We can't even tell kids at Double A. You know what they'll do to three nuts who claim they saw aliens."

Late in the afternoon Patrick's and Nick's parents arrived to pick them up. Mr. Pope had brought pizza and everyone had supper together. The boys were quiet, but the adults were too busy talking to notice.

That changed the next week. It became obvious something was wrong with these three boys. Normally, they participated in class. They were friendly with the other kids. They talked to their parents. Now, they sat quietly and stared at their desk tops. They stood silently by themselves at recess. They sat by themselves at lunch and didn't eat much. When they got home they went to their rooms. They didn't talk at supper.

Their parents noticed first and asked what was wrong. Each boy answered the same, "Nothing. Everything is fine." Nick's mother took him to his pediatrician for a checkup. Nick was perfectly healthy.

Mike's father dismissed it saying, "The kid's hormones are kicking in. He's becoming a teenager. We might as well get used it. For the next five years we're gonna be stuck with a pouting, pimply, pain in the neck."

The boys had nightmares. They cried out in their sleep and woke their parents. They were jumpy. They all wanted to sleep with a nightlight. Mike asked if he could sleep on the floor in his parents' room. His parents sighed and let him.

The kids at school noticed next. At first, they teased the boys for always standing apart. Then, the kids got mad and made fun of them. They played pranks on them.

When the boys' grades began to drop, teachers noticed. The three had always gotten straight As. Now, they were having trouble getting Bs. The teachers spoke to them and asked what was wrong. The school nurse called each one in to talk with her.

The three boys were in trouble. A dark cloud had settled over them, making it seem like they were living their lives in black and white. The color was all gone. They were keeping a secret that was too big for them, and that secret was wearing them down. Lots of people offered to help, but the boys kept quiet. They knew that telling the truth would only cause them more problems. They didn't know, but there is a name for what was happening to them. It's called depression. People with depression feel sad; they have no energy, and nothing interests them. That's what happened to the boys. They stopped their play. There was no more exploring other planets. They stopped their music. Practicing was just too much work, and it didn't make them happy anymore.

Chapter 6
The Performance

One Monday morning in January, Mike was in line entering the school with his class. He was silent and expressionless. His shoulders were rounded over and he hung his head, looking at the floor as he walked. Mr. Newcomb was proctor that day, and was standing nearby. He called Mike and asked him to step out of line.

"I recall that you, Mr. Pope and Mr. Weaver have formed a band," Mr. Newcomb said enthusiastically. "I think I have an idea you'll like. I am on the Open House planning committee. You know how you students sing the school hymn *All Hail Atlantic* at the opening assembly? I think it would be nice if you three played live music. How about you practice the song this week? You know how important Open House is to our school. There will be lots of kids visiting here with their parents, thinking about transferring in. We want to make a good impression."

Mike knew all about Open House. It happened every year. It was the way Atlantic Academy showed itself off to the community. It helped bring in new kids. Last year, Mike had been a student guide. He took families on tours of the school and answered their questions.

Mr. Newcomb's idea was magical. It pulled Mike out of his depression. For the first time in a long time he wanted to do something. Something mattered and seemed like it could be fun. At recess he met Nick and Patrick. "Band practice at my house every night this week," he said with an enthusiasm he had not experienced for months.

"I don't really feel like it?" Patrick answered, still locked in his depression. Mike told him Mr. Newcomb wanted live music for the Open House assembly.

"It's gonna be tough," said Nick, still as disinterested in life as Patrick. "We have homework every night. I don't know if my parents will drive me all over Hampton."

"You guys come home from school with me every day. Then, your parents only have to pick you up," explained Mike, trying to fire up his friends. "If they can't make it, my Dad can take you home. We'll do homework first, and then we'll practice as long as we can. It's just one song. We already know how to sing it. We only have to learn the music."

That worked. Patrick and Nick both agreed; a live performance could be fun. They pulled out of their depression as magically as Mike had. At the end of the day the three met their parents in the school parking lot and described Mr. Newcomb's idea. For the adults, this was good news. After two months of moping, they were relieved the boys were finally excited about something.

The band practiced hard and learned the music first. They agreed Mike would sing the song, while Patrick and Nick sang the back up. By the second day, the Sirens had the song nailed and practice became fun. They added some guitar riffs and drum solos. *All Hail Atlantic* began to rock. As the week wore on, it began to rock loud and hard.

Monday morning, Patrick and his father stopped by Mike's house and helped load the drums into Mrs. Castleton's van. The boys arrived at school early and set up their instruments on the gym stage. Then, they got into line with their class.

The Open House assembly started at 10:00. The janitor had prepared the gym by setting up rows of folding chairs, leaving a wide center aisle. Atlantic Academy's student body filed in, one class after another. The pre-schoolers and kindergarteners entered first and took their seats in front. Then, the higher grades arrived. The junior high kids filed in last and sat in the back rows.

Mr. Newcomb said he would reserve seats for Mike, Nick, and Patrick with the pre-schoolers, right next to the stage stairs. That way they could get to their instruments quickly and easily. As the three came in Mr. Newcomb pulled them aside. "I'm sorry boys," he said. "I've got some bad news. Mrs. Martin chairs the Open House committee. She says live music is too risky. She doesn't want anything to go wrong."

The boys' faces dropped. They knew why Mrs. Martin had pulled the plug on them, and it had nothing to do with risk. The boys had done all that practicing. They were pumped and ready to perform. Now, it was all taken away. They felt the cloud drop back over them.

"What are they gonna do instead?" asked Nick, the disappointment showing on his face.

"We have a CD player on the edge of the stage," explained Mr. Newcomb. "Mrs. Martin says it safer to play a recording of the school hymn. I'm sorry. Go to your seats."

The boys looked at the rows of chairs where their classmates were sitting. The rows were filled; there were no seats for them. They were supposed to sit up front. "There aren't any," said Patrick, pointing out the full rows to Mr. Newcomb.

"Then you'll have sit in the seats up front reserved for you," Mr. Newcomb said as he waved the boys towards the stage. "I'm really sorry," the music teacher added. "I know you're disappointed."

The boys dropped into their chairs at the front of the gym, facing the stage where they were supposed to play. The excitement was all gone. They slumped in their seats and crossed their arms over their chests. It was obvious they were disappointed - if anyone bothered to look. They glanced up at the stage where their instruments were set up, ready for their cancelled performance. Patrick had written "The

Sirens" on the bass drum. He read the name of his band and then, stared at his feet. Looking at the instruments just hurt too much. "I feel like my dog just died," Mike said.

The gym continued to fill. Visiting parents and their children came in and sat on the bleachers, right next to the boys. School workers, the janitor, the office help, Mrs. Alvarez the lunch lady, and the trustees stood along the other side of the gym.

The Atlantic Academy high school Head Master - Miss Watson's boss – went to the lectern and tested the microphone. He welcomed the visiting parents and kids. He explained Open House to the audience and told them how important it was in bringing in new students. After him, there were brief speeches by other dignitaries. Some volunteers were given awards.

To close the assembly, the students would sing the school hymn *All Hail Atlantic*. When it was time, Mrs. Martin got up from her seat and walked to the stage with a CD in hand. She put the CD in the player and pushed the button. Nothing happened. She examined the player for a while before discovering it was not plugged in. She picked up the cord and looked for the outlet. It was at the back of the stage, and the cord was obviously not long enough to reach.

The room began to stir. Feet shuffled and kids giggled. Adults whispered while Mrs. Martin looked around desperately for a solution. Mr. Smith came to her rescue. He climbed up on the stage and disappeared behind the curtain where he could be heard rummaging around.

Meanwhile, the murmur in the gym changed to laughter. This new sound caught Mike's attention. He looked up from his feet and glanced at the bleachers next to his seat. He could tell from the visitors' faces that this blunder was costing Double A their respect.

Mr. Smith found an extension cord. He plugged it into the outlet and brought the other end to Mrs. Martin. The woman was so embarrassed she had turned red. As fast as she could, she plugged in the player and pushed the play button.

The recording started, but the gym was too big a space for the small speakers. The audience could barely hear the music. Those who could hear could only make out some of the words, *All Hail Atlantic, from thy hallowed halls. I hear your sweet chorus, my spirit it calls.* Mrs. Martin raised her arms in a gesture that told the student body to join in the song. A few scattered kids who remembered the lyrics started to sing, but they quickly stopped when they realized they were singing alone.

By the green ocean's foam, you are my beloved home... Mrs. Martin waved her arms again. This time none of the students made a peep. Panic spread over the teacher's face as she looked around for help, from someone, from anyone. She was desperate. She made the gesture with her arms one more time. Again, nothing.

Mike looked up again at the visiting parents in the bleachers. Some were frowning, while others shook their heads in disappointment. He was watching Open House go down in flames. Mike elbowed Nick and Patrick. "Come on," he said. "We've gotta save this." Hunched over so as to appear as small as possible, the boys jogged up the stage stairs. The adults were so concerned with the disaster happening before their eyes they did not notice the boys go to their instruments. They didn't see Patrick sit at the drums. They didn't see Mike and Nick pick up their electric guitars and put the straps over their shoulders.

Mike placed his captain's hat on his head and cocked it to one side to show a little attitude. He put his remote pickup in his back pocket and hung his guitar from his shoulder by its fuzzy pink strap. He stepped to the front of the stage. So far, no one but the pre-schoolers and kindergartners had noticed the three boys. The little ones all watched quietly, curious to see what these junior high kids were up to.

Mike turned and gave a silent count to his friends, "One, two, three…" Patrick tapped a beat and Mike played the first cords. All three started singing *All Hail Atlantic, from thy hallowed halls. I hear your sweet chorus, my spirit it calls.*

The sound from the band's speakers was rich and strong and filled the cavernous gym. The buzz of voices stopped instantly as everyone looked toward the stage. Mike held up his arms to the student body, using the same gesture Mrs. Martin had made. The junior high kids understood what he was telling to them and they started singing. Thanks to the big speakers they could hear the words clearly. Encouraged by the junior high, the grammar school joined in.

The Sirens led the student body through the whole song. Watching the kids swaying and clapping the boys could tell they had connected with their audience. *As I stand on the Atlantic shore, I think of those who have stood here before,* the student body sang in one full, loud voice. There was no doubt; live music was far better than a CD.

Mike glanced at his band mates and whispered "Encore." The Sirens started the song again. This time, the excited students stood up. Rows of uniforms swayed back and forth as the gym full of students clapped to the beat. *As I stand on the sand, and look at the sea, I think of those who will follow me.*

Teachers weren't sure what to do. Some sang. Others looked surprised. Mrs. Martin was furious. She flushed a deep shade of red that clashed unflatteringly with her orange hair. She looked like her face might explode.

No one paid the unhappy teacher any attention. The visiting parents clapped to the beat, while their children grinned and soaked up the excitement. The visiting kids didn't know the words to the song, so they just clapped and swayed. As the song ended the second time, Mike yelled into the microphone, "One more time, Double A."

All hail Atlantic...

When the song ended the third time Mike turned to his smiling friends with a devilish look in his blue eyes. He whispered to them "Rock it." Patrick and Nick smiled and nodded. For an intro to the rock version, Patrick played a long, loud drum roll. The students stopped singing and stared in surprise. What was this? Next, Mike bent his head back and brought his guitar up onto his chest. He played a wailing solo that ended with his guitar crying like a cat as he slid his fingers up and down the strings.

"Double A. We are the Sirens. Thanks for having us here today. This one's for you," Mike yelled as the Sirens broke into their rock version of *All Hail Atlantic*. Mike crouched backward like he was sitting and began to duck walk across the stage. The duck walk is done by squatting down on one foot and holding your other foot out in front of you. Then, you hop, hop, hop. Guitar players Chuck Berry and Angus Young of AC/DC made the duck walk famous. The Atlantic Academy students were too young to know who these guys were. For them, this was just a cool move. They couldn't wait for recess when they could try duck walking around the school yard.

As the Sirens finished the rock version, Mike played a guitar solo, still doing the duck walk. At the same time, he bobbed his head up and down. The kids did not know what Mike was doing, but the visiting adults all did. They had been to AC/DC concerts when they were young. They recognized Mike's imitation of the band's famous guitar player Angus Young. They began to clap and yell "Ang-gus. Ang-gus. Ang-gus," just like they used to do at AC/DC concerts.

Still imitating Angus Young, Mike jumped down from the stage, like the famous guitarist used to do. He continued to play as he jogged up the middle aisle toward the other end of the gym. As he passed by, students reached out to touch him. When he got to the back of the gym he turned to face the stage, and began another solo. The students had all turned to watch him.

Mike did not see the red-faced Mrs. Martin move up behind him, getting into position to put a stop to his act. She was about to reach out and grab Mike when she felt a hand on her own shoulder. It was Miss Watson. The principal was so short the teacher had to lower her head to hear what Miss Watson said. "Let him finish. When it's over, tell Mr. Castleton and his friends they have detention with me after school."

Miss Watson stepped back and watched Mike, leaving Mrs. Martin puzzled and unsure what the principal was thinking. Her words had sounded angry, but the normally expressionless Miss Watson was wearing just a hint of a smile, like she had found something she had been looking for.

Unaware of what had just happened behind him, Mike finished his solo and jogged back up the aisle. He jumped onto the stage and gave Nick and

Patrick a look that said, "It's time to wrap it up." Nick and Patrick shook their heads. They wanted to do the song one more time. Mike nodded, raised his arms, and yelled into the microphone "One more time, Double A!" *All hail Atlantic……*

As the audience sang the hymn, Mike backed up to the rear of the stage. When the song ended Patrick gave a drum roll and Mike charged forward. He dropped to his knees and slid to the edge of the stage with his arms wide open. As he came to a stop he yelled at the top of his lungs "Hooray, Atlantic Academy!"

The show was over. The kids cheered and whistled while the Sirens took several bows. Teachers signaled their excited students to form a line and go back into the school. Meanwhile, the Sirens stood on the stage to catch their breath. They were dripping with sweat. Patrick looked at the clock and said to Mike and Nick "That was 20 minutes."

Mike looked again at the Open House visitors in the bleachers. He could see from the parents' faces they thought Atlantic Academy was a very creative school. The kids thought this place was awesome.

The boys walked across the empty gym to find Mrs. Martin waiting for them at the door, her face still bright red. She had been embarrassed, and she was angry. She glared at them, her arms folded across her chest. As they got near enough to hear, she spat out the words, "Miss Watson says you will serve detention in her office this afternoon after school. Be there," she hissed before she turned and stomped off.

"Oh man," groaned Patrick. "What a bummer. Why does everything have to go wrong?"

Chapter 7
Detention

After 2:45 dismissal, Nick, Mike, and Patrick met at the top of the staircase. That dark cloud was back and they were fighting to keep their depression from returning. "I've never had detention before. What will I tell my parents?" worried Patrick. "What about you guys?"

"I got sent to the office when I was in pre-school," Mike offered. "JR and I argued and threw sand at each other. We only saw the assistant principal."

"What about you, Nick?" Patrick asked. "You had detention?"

"Well, maybe a few times," Nick admitted.

Mike elbowed him and smiled. "Why, Nick, you old trouble maker, how come you never told your team mates?" Nick liked the attention and didn't confess his real story. Mrs. Martin had sentenced him to stay after school because of his unruly hair. He only spent some time with a teacher in the library. He had never been to Miss Watson's office for a real detention. So, he was just as scared as Mike and Patrick.

The boys arrived at Miss Watson's office, which consisted of two rooms, a conference room in front and her private space in back. Younger kids whispered that her private office was the torture chamber. Those that went in there were never seen again. They made some horrible screams, and then just disappeared. The boys were too old to believe those stories any more, but still dreaded getting anywhere near the back office. Most meetings were held in the conference room, as it contained a long table surrounded by chairs. Otherwise, the room was bare. There was no additional furniture, no rug, and nothing on the walls. The space was as uninviting as a police interrogation room.

Miss Watson stood in the center of the conference room and met the boys with her usual emotionless expression. Her arms were folded across her chest like Mrs. Martin's had been. "Gentlemen. Do come in, please, and be seated," she said without any welcome or warmth in her voice. The boys entered and were surprised to see Mr. Smith sitting at the far end of the table, staring at them. A stack of papers was piled next to his elbow.

"Here are three chairs," Miss Watson said. "Why don't you place them against the corridor wall so we can see each other?" The principal's instructions were expressed as a polite suggestion. Her stern voice made her intentions clear. She had given the boys an order, and they did as told without hesitation. Mike sat in the chair at the end of the row, near the table. The boys felt like suspects being questioned by the police. All that was missing was a bright light.

The boys were alone with the principal they feared and the odd teacher they laughed at. It was very uncomfortable. They slid their butts forward in their chairs and hunched their shoulders. They looked like turtles, pulling their heads into their shells. The boys would prefer to shrink into nothing and disappear. If that wasn't possible, they wanted to become the smallest targets possible.

Miss Watson remained in the middle of the room, her arms still crossed. "Well, that was quite a show you three put on," she said. "Am I correct that you were told not to perform?" They all nodded, as much as their turtle necks would allow. "Yet, you went ahead and did it anyway," she continued. "Permit me to show you the results of your performance." She stepped in front of Mr. Smith and picked up the stack of papers. She walked to the other end of the table and dropped the stack next to Mike's elbow.

"Gentlemen, we received this pile from the parents who were visiting today." The short principal's stern face broke into a smile. It was the first time the boys had ever seen this happen. "This is a stack of applications for next year. Atlantic Academy does not have room for so many children. We will have to start a waiting list."

The boys had never seen Miss Watson so excited and happy. They thought she might start to dance. "A couple of more years like this and the trustees will build the new classrooms I have been asking for," she said smiling.

"Mr. Pope, Mr. Weaver, Mr. Castleton. You have two more years at Atlantic Academy middle school. I am asking your band to play the next two

Open Houses. I will use your music to attract more students."

"Yeah, sure," Patrick agreed, his voice full of hesitation as he turned to look at Nick and then Mike. Both nodded and let out a silent sigh of relief. For the first time the boys saw a glimmer of hope; maybe they would make it out of here in one piece. They looked up at the principal, their eyes asking if the meeting was over. "No," said Miss Watson, reading their minds. "We have something else to talk about.

"How should I express this so you understand?" she asked, putting her hand on her chin. After a brief pause to ponder she began, "Mr. Smith is not really a school teacher, and I am not really a principal." The boys' foreheads furrowed in confusion.

"That didn't work," she said, noticing their expressions. She asked, "Do you know what an agent is?"

"Do you mean like CIA or FBI?" asked Nick with his usual worried expression.

"Similar to that, yes," Mr. Smith replied, speaking for the first time. He sounded different. Normally, he was confused and slightly goofy. Now, it was like he was in charge. "Miss Watson and I are agents." He smoothed his thin mustache with the tip of his index finger.

The adults gave the boys a moment to ponder this news. "How can you be?" asked Patrick. "Agents are always fighting and doing really daring stuff. That's why they're big, strong guys like James Bond."

"No." replied Mr. Smith. "An agent's role is to fit in, to go unnoticed. A flashy hero can't do that. You only succeed if you look ordinary."

"That's not all you wanted to say, is it?" Mike asked Miss Watson. "You've got more to tell us, don't you?"

"Yes," the tiny Principal replied. "We plan to give this to you in small pieces. You couldn't handle everything at once. We are agents, and we are on a mission," she added. "Our mission is to find you three."

Miss Watson was right. This was more than the boys could get their heads around. They wiggled in their chairs, shuffled their feet, and looked at each other. "Why us?" asked Nick. "What do you want us for?"

"To find someone," said Mr. Smith. "To find someone very important to us."

"Maybe it would be best if you gave it to us all at once, rather than in pieces," Mike interjected. "I mean, I'm not getting it this way."

Mr. Smith shrugged. "As you wish." He stroked his mustache several times before beginning. "We are agents and we are on a mission to find three young people. Their job will be to find someone for us and to stop him from doing something terrible." The boys stared with their mouths hanging open. The story still didn't make sense.

"Remember agents have to blend in," Mr. Smith continued. "If we leave the school, Miss Watson and I will stick out. People will know we are not what we pretend to be. We are hiding here at Atlantic Academy and we can't risk going outside the school. So, we need someone else to do our mission for us. You are the best kids for the job. That is why we chose you."

The boys' mouths were still open. Mike finally asked, "Why can't you go out of the school? Other teachers do."

"Because we do not come from here," Miss Watson said. "We don't know all the little details of daily life in Hampton. They will give us away. If we give ourselves away, there will be lots of questions, and lots of problems."

The boys continued to stare at the adults in confusion and disbelief. "Alright. I will lay it all out for you," Mr. Smith snapped, annoyed that the boys had not understood him. "If you can't handle it, too bad. We'll start all over again and find someone else. Time is something we have plenty of.

"We are agents," he repeated, speaking forcefully and rapidly. "We are looking for a team that will find someone for us. They will stop him from doing what he plans to do. We chose you because we are not from here." The boys remained confused. Mr. Smith had repeated the same information they could not understand, or believe the first time.

Mr. Smith paused and drew his finger tip along his mustache several times. Then, he added an important piece to the story. "At least we are not from here now. We are from the future. We are time travelers."

That was too much for poor Patrick. He looked at Miss Watson and asked "Are you guys making a joke? Is this one of those hidden camera shows?" His brain was swirling. None of this made sense. Was it possible Miss Watson was not really a school principal? No. That was crazy. Were she and the goofy Social Studies teacher really agents from the future? Even more crazy.

"Can you prove it?" asked Nick. He shook his head side-to-side. "This can't be real. This just can't be real," his mind repeated over and over,

"Yes, we can prove it," replied Mr. Smith. "And we will."

Mike looked at the teacher that was not a teacher and raised his eyebrows, an expression that said, "Go ahead."

"Not right away," Miss Watson replied. "We still have more to tell you."

"Why us?" Patrick broke in. "If this guy is going to do something really bad, why don't you tell the government? The president? The CIA?"

"If the government learned that we time travel, they would want our technology," Mr. Smith replied. "They would not help us. They would lock us up and question us. An agent can't carry out a mission in a jail cell." Muttering his frustration under his breath he added, "It's hard enough to do it locked up in a school."

"Why not ask some adults?" Mike asked. "We're just kids in the sixth grade. I could ask my Dad to help you." The other two nodded. Yes, their fathers. They could do the job far better.

"You are still young and open minded. What did you think when we told you we were from the future?" asked Miss Watson. "You didn't believe us," she replied, answering her own question. "How do you think adults would react?"

The boys nodded. Yeah. Adults are pretty closed minded. If they told this news to their fathers, they would react like Mike's dad when they reported seeing UFOs. Their fathers would think it was a game. Nope. The boys couldn't think of anyone else for the job. They were stuck with it. It was fun to dream about space and science fiction, but this was scary. Each boy had a headache.

The adults knew the boys were on overload. "Gentlemen, let's take a break," said Mr. Smith. "I'll give you that proof you asked for. We'll show you our time craft. We can get back to the mission later."

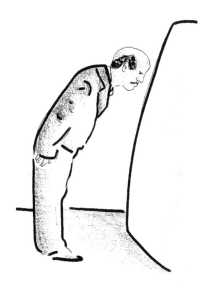

Chapter 8

The Time Craft of the Roof

Mr. Smith opened the office door and led the boys out into the corridor. Miss Watson brought up the rear. Mike noticed she had not closed her door and knew what that meant. They would be returning to the dreaded conference room.

The corridor was empty and all the classrooms were closed. It appeared everyone had left for the night. No. The lunch lady, Mrs. Alvarez opened the kitchen door. She backed out, pulling a mop and bucket after her. She had just finished cleaning for the day. Like Mr. Smith and Miss Watson, Mrs. Alvarez was a tiny woman, about the same age as the principal and the teacher.

Mrs. Alvarez stood motionless in front of the open kitchen door and stared at the boys as they walked by. She nodded to Mr. Smith and smiled at Miss Watson. The boys did not see these looks, or they would have wondered how much Mrs. Alvarez knew.

Mr. Smith turned left and led the group up the middle stair case. On the second floor, he turned left again and walked towards the back of the school. The short parade arrived at a steel fire door next to the Boys Room. Mike, Patrick, and Nick knew this door, as they passed it several times a day. They always guessed it was a closet that contained some equipment, or school supplies.

Mr. Smith took a key from his pocket and unlocked the door. He tugged hard to pull it open, indicating the door had not been used for some time. The boys were not going where no one had gone before, but no one went there often.

Mr. Smith turned on a light to reveal a set of stairs. The stairs led to only one place – the roof. Mr. Smith climbed the stairs and at the top, pushed open a trap door. Sunlight and cold January air poured in.

The tiny Social Studies teacher stepped onto the roof and the others followed.

The boys looked around. The roof was flat and covered with tar and small pebbles. Here and there, were patches of snow. The only objects on the roof were a couple of large sheet metal boxes and a chimney. "This way," said Mr. Smith. He walked as if he was headed to something, but there was nothing there. The man stopped abruptly. "Here," he said. "Miss Watson, can you give me a hand?" Miss Watson walked past Mr. Smith, about the length of a car, and turned to face him. The two reached down at the same time and with their hands felt for something. When they had found it, each took hold.

"Ready?" asked Mr. Smith.

"Yes."

"Then, one, two, three…"

What words best describe the boys' reaction? Surprise? Awe? Shock? None of these words do the job. It was like someone had just punched them. The boys backed up stumbling. Nick and Mike gasped. Patrick made a sound like "awwwww." A craft had appeared before their eyes. It only took a second for them to realize they had seen this craft before. Fear swept over them.

"I know this thing," Mike said, his voice shaking.

"You do?" asked Mr. Smith with surprise.

"We saw it in the woods," Mike continued, still upset and frightened.

"You did?" asked Miss Watson with even more surprise.

"What are you guys doing with it?" asked Patrick.

"Yeah." Nick added, his face looking more worried that usual. "What's it doing here?"

Miss Watson and Mr. Smith stared at the boys in stunned disbelief. "Let's go back to the beginning," said Mr. Smith. "How do you know this craft?"

"We saw it in the woods, along with another one. There were six aliens. Three gray and three green," Patrick replied.

"Oh no!" said Miss Watson putting her hand to her mouth. "Have you told anyone?"

"No," Patrick answered. "Yeah," he corrected. "We told Mike's father, but he didn't believe us."

"You have told no one else?" Mr. Smith asked again. His tone was dead serious. "You saw two craft and six aliens, and you have not told anyone else?"

"I said no," repeated Patrick, a little annoyed at the persistent questioning. "We kept it secret. We didn't want anyone to think we were crazy. Instead, we went crazy. We were scared. We had nightmares."

"I am so sorry," Miss Watson said compassionately. "Now I understand why your grades dropped after November. You were frightened. You did not understand what you had seen."

"I too am so sorry," Mr. Smith added. "You did not see aliens. You saw us. We have been careless. We thought no one could get to those woods. We thought it safe to have our meetings there."

"It didn't look like you guys," Nick said. "Who were the others?"

"I'll explain later why we didn't look like we do now," Mr. Smith answered. "The others were another team. They were bringing us information. We're amazed you found a way to get into those woods. We're amazed you saw us. We're amazed you kept it a secret all this time. There is no doubt; you are just the team we need. Imagine, when your grades dropped, we started to look for other kids."

The teacher and principal were sorry for having frightened the boys. The boys were just glad to know they were not crazy. Finally, someone believed them. They quickly forgot their two month nightmare.

Recovered from the shock of seeing the craft again, they wondered how Mr. Smith and Miss

Watson had made it appear. Some sort of cloth had covered it. Now, that cloth was lying on the roof in front of them. However, only some of the cover was there. More precisely, there were places where there was fabric, while in other places they saw the roof. It was like there were huge holes in the material that they could see through.

Mr. Smith noticed them staring at the crumpled cloth that was half there and half not. "It's a covering," he explained. "Where you see fabric you are looking at the inside. Where you see nothing, you are looking at the outside. That's because you are actually seeing through the cloth. It is a cloak. It keeps our craft from being seen. This craft has been here on the school roof longer than you have attended Atlantic Academy, and no one has known it.

"Do you want to see inside?" he asked. The boys nodded. Mr. Smith put his face up to the craft's hull and squinted, like he was reading something very small. He said, "Seventeen." A door opened silently, like on a minivan, only it disappeared into the craft's wall.

Miss Watson stepped in. The boys followed. Mr. Smith was last. He put his face close to the inside wall and said, "Twenty three." The door closed. Still staring at the wall he said, "X minus two." This time nothing happened. "I just turned on the cloak," he explained. "We wouldn't want anyone to spot the craft while we are showing it to you. We can only turn on the cloak from inside. Crews hope the laboratory will come up with a way to do that when we get out. Covering a craft with that cloth cloak is a pain."

The boys examined the craft's interior. There were pairs of porthole windows on both sides, with bench seats under the portholes. There were two flat windows in the front – the wall Mr. Smith had just spoken to. They allowed the pilot to see. They didn't remember any windows on the outside.

"Where are the instruments?" Patrick asked. "How do you fly this thing?"

"It has a mental interface," explained Mr. Smith. "The pilot's mind does all the work."

So, Mr. Smith and Miss Watson had been telling the truth after all. This was unbelievable, but there was no denying it was true. The boys were in a craft that used an advanced technology and appeared to come from the future. Miss Watson and Mr. Smith gave them time to think.

"Are all UFOs time craft?" Mike asked. "Have all those UFOs people see been you guys?"

"Yes. UFOs are time craft," Mr. Smith answered. "No, Miss Watson and I have not been the crews. In the future there is a whole fleet of craft like this. They are always traveling back in time. Every now and then a crew gets careless and they are spotted, like we were seen by you."

"You mean there are others like you, and they are here a lot?" asked Nick.

"Yes," replied Mr. Smith, stroking his upper lip with his forefinger.

"Why? What are you doing?" Nick wondered. "Are you always on missions?"

"We called ourselves agents because you understand that word," added Miss Watson. "In our time we are known as a Fixer team. When another team slips up and alters time, we fix the problem. We prevent something we call *Chaos.* It is not the same thing you think of when you hear that word."

"I think we should wrap up for today," said Mr. Smith. "You boys have absorbed a lot. I know it's been hard and you need some time to think. A good night's sleep will probably help." He turned and again placed his face against the wall. "Square root three," he said, causing the door to open silently.

The boys waited as Miss Watson and Mr. Smith covered the craft with the fabric cloak. They watched the craft disappear as the cloth was pulled over it. The craft was there one moment, and then it was gone. Nick thought to himself, "That cover is a pain in the neck. There has to be a better way."

"Gentlemen," Mr. Smith said to the small group on the school roof. "Tomorrow, I want you to report for detention again. Miss Watson and I will explain the mission to you and answer all your questions. First, I have something to ask," he continued. "You kept your secret for two months. Please, do not tell anyone what we have shown you. Miss Watson and I do not want to fix any more problems. This mission is critical. We expect you to talk to each other about it. However, speak only face-to-face, when you are sure no one else is around. Please use your heads."

He led the group back to the trap door. Inside he said, "Gentlemen, it will be best to split up. Please go to your lockers and get your coats and backpacks. Then, take the rear stairs and leave the building by the gym. Miss Watson, I will return to my classroom for a while. For appearance sake, it would be best if you spent some time in your office."

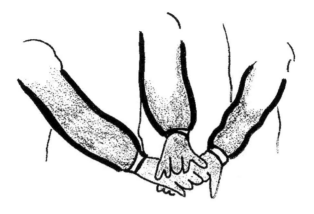

Chapter 9
The Decision

Patrick's father waited in the parking lot along with Mike's and Nick's mothers. You can imagine their rides home. Their parents thought the boys had been in detention and the boys would have to tell them there was another detention tomorrow. There was only one good thing. Their parents were not upset about the reasons for the punishment. A live version of *All Hail Atlantic,* a Rock and Roll version, and an Angus Young impersonation seemed pretty innocent.

Patrick's father told him to use his head next time. Atlantic Academy was a private school and rules were important. Mike's mother thought the story was funny. Nick's younger brother and sister had been at the performance and had told their mother how great it was. Mrs. Pope was proud, not angry. Nick had broken the rules, so she couldn't tell him she was proud. Instead, she gave him an extra-long hug and a kiss.

Even if their parents were okay with the detentions, the boys still bore a heavy burden. They had been asked to take on a dangerous job. This wasn't science fiction. This was real. They had been in a time craft. They knew two people from the future.

That night, Mike texted Patrick and Nick. *u there?* he asked.

Yes, the other two answered.
What r u doing?
Thinking, wrote Patrick.
Same, replied Nick.
We need to talk.
Not this way, warned Nick.
Tomorrow. Recess. By the tree. Patrick wrote.
OK, both Mike and Nick replied. *ttyl.*

At morning recess, the three met in the playground at the tree near the sand box. "I didn't sleep last night," said Mike.

"I didn't get much either," Nick added.

"What are we gonna do?" asked Patrick.

"We wanted to go into space and be the first people on Mars," Mike argued. "We don't know anything about this job. We don't even know where we'd be going. They mentioned earth and time travel, but I haven't heard anything about space. I wanted to be an astronaut, not a secret agent, or a Fixer."

Nick thought a moment. "Yeah, but we want to be astronauts because we want adventure. I'm scared, but I don't want to miss out on something really exciting."

"It could be the chance of a lifetime," thought Patrick out loud. "But we all go together. You guys are my best friends. If they won't take both of you, I won't go either. It's no deal."

"Okay," Mike said with determination. "We all agree? We meet with Miss Watson and Mr. Smith again, and we hear what they have to say?" The other two nodded. "We won't make up our minds until then. All for one, and one for all. They take all of us, or they don't get any of us." Mike reached out his hand

and the others placed theirs on top of his to seal their promise.

"See you guys at the middle staircase at 2:45," Patrick said. The bell rang and they got in line with their class.

After dismissal the boys met again at the top of the stairs. Yesterday, they dreaded going to Miss Watson's office. It was easier this time. They knew they weren't being punished. They would listen to the adults. At the end, they would make up their minds and give them their answer. They would all go on the mission, or no one would. Mr. Smith and Miss Watson would have to find someone else. After all, Mr. Smith had said he had plenty of time, whatever that meant.

They found Miss Watson waiting for them, just like the day before. Again, she waved them into her conference room without any warmth or emotion. Yesterday, the boys had sat up against the wall like prisoners facing a firing squad. Today, Miss Watson invited them to sit at the conference table. They realized what this gesture meant. She was treating them as equals.

Mike and Nick sat at the side of the long table. Patrick sat on the end so he was facing Mr. Smith.

Miss Watson sat next to the Social Studies teacher. "How was your night, gentlemen?" the principal asked, her face still expressionless.

"Not very good," said Patrick. "I didn't sleep." The others nodded in agreement. "We had a lot to think about. Do you two know how hard this is?" he asked the small adults.

"Yes, we do," Miss Watson answered. "That is why we ended yesterday's meeting. You needed time to think. You also needed time to talk to each other. I'm guessing you used recess to do that. I noticed you by the tree."

"Yes," Patrick replied. "We're ready to hear you out. Then, we'll give you our answer. You need to know up front that it is all of us, or none of us."

"Fair enough," replied Miss Watson. She didn't smile, but she was pleased that Patrick had stood up to her. She had noticed that he sat at the end of the table. He would speak for them all, and he was bargaining like an adult. He would make a good team leader. Things were moving along just fine.

"I want to start with some history," Miss Watson began. "Well, it's history for us. It's the future for you." Yesterday, Miss Watson's words would have confused the boys. This time, they did not even blink.

"A few years from now, a scientific summit will take place in Hampton. One of the most important people in history will speak here." The boys raised their eyebrows in surprise. It was hard to believe anything noteworthy would occur in a town as small as Hampton.

"It will happen at the Oakwood, the hotel on the beach," Miss Watson continued. "Dr. James A. MacDonald of the University of New Hampshire will give the world a new type of seed. Grain and cereal plants will grow so fast no one will be hungry again. The rest of the plants will become bio-fuels. The energy crisis will be over, forever."

Miss Watson paused while the boys pondered that. "Gentlemen," she asked. "Can you imagine what this world would be like if no one was hungry? Can you imagine so much food that it costs almost nothing to feed a family? Can you imagine abundant, non-polluting energy everywhere? Can you imagine a world where no one fights over food or energy? Can you imagine a world where no one can use food or energy to control or harm others?"

The boys couldn't imagine it. They lived in a rich country. They had never been hungry in their lives. Sometimes their parents complained about the price of food or gasoline. Still, their refrigerators were always full. They always had gas in their cars.

"Hunger is hard to imagine if you have never seen it," the principal continued, giving an understanding nod to their silence. "For most of history there was no steady supply of food. Even today, lots of people struggle to get enough to eat. They can't buy fuel for heat or for cooking.

"Hunger is a waste of human ability. People can't change the world if they spend all their time looking for food. Get rid of hunger and people can focus on other things, like making the world a better place. That is what happened after the Hampton Summit. Days later, scientists had made the new seeds. Days after that, plants were growing. Crops were harvested in two months. Some seed was planted again. The rest went into empty bellies all over the world. In two years, bio-fuel factories popped up everywhere. Every city, town, and village, in every country made its own cheap energy from leftover plants.

"Poor families saved money and sent their children to school. Those children became teachers, scientists, doctors, and artists. Meanwhile, gentlemen," she continued. "The world grew so wealthy money was unimportant. How do you know someone is rich? The rich own more. They go more places. They do more things. If everyone can do the same, money doesn't matter.

"A peaceful world makes a lot of progress. We learned to time travel," Miss Watson continued. "We use time travel to study the past. It allows us to go back and watch history first hand."

"So that's what people do in the future?" asked Patrick. "You study us? Doesn't that get a little old?"

"Only a few of us time travel," Miss Watson explained. "We do it to help scholars. Mr. Smith and I work for the Time Institute. The Institute has a fleet of time craft. Institute crews fly the craft and make the observations."

"Okay, we get it," Patrick responded, continuing to speak for his friends. "The question is, what do you want us to do? We're not historians or anything. The other question is, why us? Why do you want us for this mission?"

"Let's start with *Why you?*" said Mr. Smith rocking back in his chair, his hands behind his head. "The answer is easy. Guts."

"Let me express that more delicately," Miss Watson said. "We need a team of three people, each with special aptitudes. We need a pilot who can do math quickly and easily. It really helps if he or she is a natural leader. You Mr. Weaver, have those two aptitudes. We need an observer that is good in science. The job is called science observer. We shorten it to S/O. Mr. Castleton; you will make a good S/O. Finally, things go wrong. It's a problem if a crew is in the past and its craft breaks down. So, every team has an engineer to repair the craft and the equipment. Mr. Pope, I've watched you in the computer lab. I know that you and your grandfather restored an antique sports car. You have the aptitude to be an engineer.

"We didn't make a snap decision yesterday when I gave you detention. Mr. Smith and I have been watching you since pre-school. There are other students who have the same aptitudes you have. However, they don't have what Mr. Smith called *guts*."

"So, we were right," Patrick said. "You were watching us this year. Why this year? Why didn't you wait until we were older?"

"Yes," Miss Watson answered. "We have been watching you. You're at the best age for us. You're old enough to handle responsibility, but if we wait another year, you may grow. We need you the size you are right now.

"Yesterday," she continued "you boys showed us the final quality we need. Gentlemen, you are audacious. That word means daring. In other words, guts. You came to the school's rescue and you pulled off an amazing success. That answers your question Mr. Weaver, *Why you?*

"Your other question was *What do you want us to do?* As I described, our world -humanity's future - is wonderful, but it's in danger. That is why this mission. We need you to find someone, and we need you to stop him," continued Miss Watson. "His name is Dr. Roger Morley, and he was our colleague at the Time Institute. He is a brilliant S/O, teacher, and researcher. His students loved him."

"Dr. Morley developed a brain tumor. Surgeons removed it and everyone thought he would be fine. However, it has grown back and has affected his mind. He wants to take over the world and become its dictator."

"Morley talked a maintenance crew into helping him," added Mr. Smith. "One of them got cold feet and told us Morley's plan. That's how we know what he's up to."

"Minions," Mike blurted. Everyone looked at him and wondered what he meant. "Minions," explained Mike. "In the movies, every evil genius who tries to take over the world has minions. They're usually dumb, just bad guys with muscle."

Miss Watson waited patiently for Mike to finish. "The other two men stole a time craft for Dr. Morley," she continued. "They have gone back in time to stop Dr. James MacDonald before the Hampton Summit."

Mr. Smith added an important but chilling detail. "Dr. Morley will commit the worst crime in history. He plans to stop Dr. MacDonald by *murdering* Dr. MacDonald. They are going to assassinate him." The boys' mouths dropped opened. This job kept getting worse. They squirmed in their chairs.

"Mr. Smith and I cannot do this mission," Miss Watson continued. "We stand out too much. You don't have that problem. You know the town and you know the people. You have the aptitudes. You are the best choice for us."

"Can he do that?" asked Nick, disbelief added to his normal worried expression. "Kill Dr. MacDonald? I mean, like isn't the future what it is?"

"The Grandfather Paradox," Mike blurted out again. This time, the boys didn't bother to ask what he meant. They just waited for him to explain. "If you go back in time and kill your grandfather before he marries your grandmother, your father will never be born. You will never be born," Mike told his friends.

"How do you know about the Grandfather Paradox?" asked Miss Watson, surprise on her face.

"My father reads all these science magazines. He told me about it," replied Mike. "He gives me puzzles like this to think about."

"It obviously works," muttered Mr. Smith as he passed his finger tip over his mustache.

"So, if Morley kills MacDonald, the future you know will never exist," Mike concluded.

"Oh, worse than that," Miss Watson replied, shaking her head with a worried expression. "You need to know this, because it affects you. If Dr. Morley kills Dr. MacDonald something horrible happens, something we call Chaos. The Hampton Summit is only a couple of years away. Most of the people alive right now will be hurt. It will change your futures and the futures of all your families."

The boys wiggled nervously. "Why would he do this?" asked Nick.

"We're not sure what he's thinking," Miss Watson replied. "Remember. He's insane. We suspect he will create Chaos to take control. We don't know how."

"Gentlemen," Mr. Smith interrupted impatiently. There had been enough talking and he was ready to force the issue. "We need your decision. Will you do the mission?"

Patrick glanced from Mike to Nick, trying to read his friends' faces. Nick looked even more worried than normal, but he gave a slight nod. Patrick looked at Mike. Mike didn't look enthusiastic, but shrugged his shoulders as if to say, "If Nick's going, I guess I will too."

"One for all, and all for one." Patrick said, holding out his hand. With grim expressions Nick and Mike placed theirs on his.

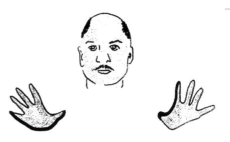

Chapter 10
Time Travel

"When do we leave?" asked Patrick. He figured he would explain the trip to his parents, pack, and say goodbye.

Mr. Smith stood up. "In the future we have a saying," he replied with a smile. "There is no time like the present."

This caught the boys by surprise and they started to chatter at once. Mr. Smith held up his hands to calm them. "We will leave now and return to this very moment. No one will ever know you left the school. You will all meet your parents at 4:00, right on schedule." The boys looked at the clock. It was 3:35.

Once again, the boys followed their principal and teacher to the roof, lost in thought. If they wanted to be heroes, this was a bad deal. If they succeeded, they would return to this very moment. No one would ever know they had gone. No one would ever know what they had done. Nothing would change.

Nothing would change unless they blew the mission. Even then, no one would recognize any difference. History would go on being bloody and violent. No one would guess that there could have been a peaceful future, if three 12-year old boys had not failed. So, there would be no medals, no ceremonies. There was only the terrifying responsibility that had just settled on their shoulders.

On the roof, Miss Watson and Mr. Smith removed their craft's cloak and folded it. Mr. Smith opened the door and stepped in. He looked back and asked, "Mr. Pope, Mr. Castleton, will you join me?"

"What about Patrick?" Mike asked with concern.

"Mr. Weaver will follow in the next flight," Miss Watson answered reassuringly. "You see, the craft can only carry a crew of three. Mr. Smith will take you two now. Then, he will return for Mr. Weaver and me. During your trip Mr. Smith will explain the jobs of science observer and engineer to you. These are things you need to know. On the second trip we will explain the pilot's role to Mr. Weaver."

Mike still looked puzzled. "Will you guys just hang around on the roof waiting while we're gone?" he asked.

"Mr. Smith will return to this moment," Miss Watson replied. "We will see the door close and reopen. You and Mr. Pope will be there when it closes. When it opens, there will only be Mr. Smith. You will meet us at the arrival/departure pad where Mr. Smith leaves you. You will see the same thing happen. The door will close on just Mr. Smith. When it opens, Mr. Weaver and I will be there." Mike wasn't sure he understood, but he was satisfied and stepped into the craft.

"It's a time travel thing," Mr. Smith added. "Time travel messes with your mind. That's something you're going hear a lot. I wish I could say you'll get used to it, but you won't. None of us do. Have a seat," he instructed Mike and Nick, pointing at the low benches on each side of the craft. "We will be in flight for what will seem about fifteen minutes, although there is really no passage of time while you're traveling through it." The small social Studies teacher put his face up to the wall and said "Eighty-one." The door closed. Still intently studying the wall Mr. Smith said, "X cubed minus two. Cloak is on."

Next, he did something strange. Keeping his face at the wall, Mr. Smith said out loud, "IC + U(2). *I see you too.* That was a good one," he added laughing. A small touch screen appeared in the wall and Mr. Smith made some selections. The boys figured he was programming the flight.

Next, Mr. Smith opened a door under one of the benches. He took out three piles of neatly folded gray clothes and stripped down to his shorts and tee shirt. The boys were a bit embarrassed, but waited to see what he did next. Mr. Smith pulled on a pair of pants and a shirt that he took from one of the piles. They looked like a sweat suit with tight cuffs. Finally, the teacher sat on a bench and pulled on something that looked like slipper socks.

Three small items remained in the pile. The boys could see that two of them were gloves. The other one looked like a ski mask. They figured it was a head cover. Mr. Smith placed the three pieces on the corner of the bench so they were right behind him while piloting.

"You two should change into your uniforms," Mr. Smith advised.

"Is that what these are, uniforms?" asked Mike.

"Yes, but they're much more than that," the pilot explained. "When we go into space, they're gravity suits. They keep us from floating around the craft. In an accident, they can keep someone alive in space long enough to be rescued. Of course, you have to be wearing the complete suit. That's why I left the head cover and gloves where I can grab them quickly. Good safety tip."

Nick and Mike were a bit uncomfortable as they took off their school uniforms. They had never undressed in front of each other. They had never undressed in front of an adult. Mr. Smith understood and turned away while the boys put on their uniforms.

"Mr. Smith, I have been wondering about something," Mike said. Mr. Smith nodded. "You said if Dr. Morley changes history he will cause this thing you call Chaos." Mr. Smith nodded again. "If a time crew is standing around watching history happen, how can they not change it?"

"You're right. We would change history if we were there," Mr. Smith replied. "The solution is to not be there."

"Huh?" the boys asked at the same time.

Mr. Smith brought his right hand up to his chest. When he touched his chest, he disappeared. At least, most of him did. His head and two hands stayed behind suspended in space. The boys were so scared they both turned white. They pushed themselves backward across the bench, like they were trying to get away. "Don't be afraid," said Mr. Smith's head. He had not expected the boys to panic and tried to calm Nick and Mike with his hands. It might have worked if his hands were connected to some arms. One of Mr. Smith's floating hands moved to where his chest should have been. He reappeared and the boys had a whole teacher again.

"I need to be more careful when I show Mr. Weaver these suits," he said thoughtfully. "Gentlemen, our uniforms are made of the same cloth as the craft's cloak. They can be made invisible. When we have the gloves and head covers on, no one can see us. For people in the past, we're not there. So, we don't change history. We do have to be careful. We can't make any noise or bump anyone."

The boys were still white, and still shaking, so Mr. Smith spoke soothingly, "Invisibility is an old technology. Even in your time, scientists were getting close." This seemed to work. Mike and Nick stopped holding their chests, even though they still struggled to catch their breath.

"Our uniforms are gray," Mr. Smith continued. "That shows we are a Fixer team. Mapper,

Researcher, Maintenance, Administration, Security, and Teacher uniforms are all different colors. So, our uniforms are very important to us," he said reassuringly "They create artificial gravity. They save us if we're lost in space. They make us invisible. They're also comfortable, and I think I look pretty good in one." He struck a pose like a fashion model. This worked. Nick and Mike grinned weakly.

Mr. Smith stepped to the front of the craft and examined the wall. Turning back to the boys, he raised his eyebrows and announced, "Gentlemen, we have arrived." Mr. Smith opened the craft's door and stepped out, gesturing to the boys to follow. Mike and Nick found themselves standing in the middle of a large, flat area about the size of a football field. They guessed it was the arrival/departure pad Miss Watson had mentioned. A long hanger with its doors open stood a short distance away. Inside the hanger the boys could see a row of craft like Mr. Smith's. They could see people in the building working on the craft.

The arrival/departure pad was surrounded by tall buildings, so the boys knew they were in the middle of a city. "Where are we?" asked Nick.

"Welcome to the Time Institute," replied Mr. Smith.

"Yes, but where are we?" repeated Nick. "Where is this place?"

"You are in Durham, New Hampshire," Mr. Smith answered. "This is the University of New Hampshire. The Time Institute is part of UNH. It was built here to honor Dr. MacDonald."

"No way!" exclaimed Nick with disbelief. "My father takes me to UNH for hockey games. UNH is in the country, not in a city. Where are the woods and fields?"

"UNH has grown a bit since your hockey days Mr. Pope," replied Mr. Smith. "The Time Institute has made Durham an important place."

Mike looked at the city around him and observed there were no utility poles or wires. There were no advertising signs. He noticed how clean the air was. He had only experienced air this clean in the mountains, or at the beach.

"I am returning to Atlantic Academy," Mr. Smith explained to the boys. "Miss Watson and Mr. Weaver are waiting for me on the roof." He climbed back into the craft, waved at Nick and Mike, and closed the door.

Chapter 11

The Team Leader

Standing on the school roof Patrick and Miss Watson watched the craft's door close on Mr. Smith, Nick, and Mike. It reopened and Mr. Smith was by himself. "Wow, it never even moved," exclaimed Patrick with surprise.

"Mr. Smith is an experienced pilot," explained Miss Watson. "New pilots are not as smooth. When they do this you will see the craft shift a bit."

Mr. Smith stepped out. "Why don't you change Miss Watson?" he asked. "Mr. Weaver and I will wait out here." Miss Watson nodded and stepped into the craft. Mr. Smith turned to look at the soccer field below. Patrick knew he was giving Miss Watson her privacy and did the same.

"I'm ready," Miss Watson said as she stepped out of the craft.

"Mr. Weaver," Mr. Smith instructed "you will find a pile of clothes inside like those Miss Watson and I are wearing. We'll wait while you change. Let us know when you're ready. Put your head cover and the gloves with ours. We want them nearby in an emergency."

Patrick found the pile of clothes and changed. He rolled his school uniform into a bundle and placed his gloves and head cover next to the others. "Ready," he said as he stepped onto the roof, where he placed his rolled up clothes next to the chimney. If he made it back, he would need them then.

The three stepped into the craft. "Twenty three," said Mr. Smith looking at the wall. The door closed. "Pi times root four," he said next. "Mr. Weaver, pay close attention. I've just turned on the cloak."

"Yeah," Patrick said. "I've wondered. What do you do when you talk to the wall?"

"I'm operating the craft," replied Mr. Smith. "I'm reading a small screen here near the door. We have a weight limit, so the screen has to be small. The pilot can read a small screen as well a large one. The craft has a mental interface. It's operated by brain waves coming from someone solving math problems."

"That's why you keeping saying things that sound like the answers to math questions," said Patrick. He was beginning to see how he fit in.

"Yes," replied Mr. Smith. "People with the aptitude for math make stronger brain waves when they solve a math problem. You have that aptitude."

"But I'm just beginning algebra," said Patrick. "Why wouldn't a college kid be better for the job?"

"The level of math doesn't matter," Mr. Smith replied. "You only need the aptitude. All the craft does is make you use your brain. If you were in kindergarten, it could ask you to add $2 + 2$ and you would make the required brain waves."

Mr. Smith continued, "Besides a math aptitude, we need a leader. You are. We need someone who is audacious. All three of you are. Finally, that person has to weigh less than 100 pounds.

"I'll explain later," said Mr. Smith "First, we should get going. Would you like to start the craft?" He stepped aside so Patrick could take his place. Standing close to the wall, Patrick saw a screen smaller than on a cell phone. "See the math problem?" Mr. Smith asked. "Just answer it out loud."

Patrick read the following problem: R(D +1 +1). "Distribute," Patrick said to himself. "RD + R + R." He paused. "RD R R?" Then, Patrick giggled, "Hardy har, har. That is so lame! I can't believe how stupid that is."

"It may be," said Mr. Smith with a grin. "But it worked." A small touch pad appeared in the wall and he programmed it for the Time Institute, where Nick and Mike were waiting.

"That dumb joke was on *The Simpsons*," Patrick said. "The show where Bart changes his grades and ends up in a school for smart kids."

"I didn't know it had been around that long," Mr. Smith replied with surprise. "It's always been one of my favorites."

"Why didn't it ask me something serious, like a circumference divided by its diameter?" Patrick asked.

"Starting the craft requires brain waves made by math humor," shrugged Mr. Smith. "Opening and closing the door uses addition or subtraction. Turning the cloak on and off always uses exponents."

"Mike and Nick can do those problems," Patrick persisted.

"Mr. Castleton or Mr. Pope could make the craft work, sometimes," Mr. Smith explained. "But, their brain waves are not strong enough to make the craft work every time."

Patrick continued his questioning. "What's this about a weight limit?"

"This craft flies at hyper-light speed," Miss Watson replied. "It has tremendous power, but it can only move a limited amount of weight that fast. The craft and crew cannot weigh more than 400 pounds, all together."

"I'm 90 pounds," Patrick said to the small teacher and principal. "We're all about the same size."

"I weigh 110," responded Mr. Smith.

"There are two things you never ask a woman, Mr. Weaver. Her age or her weight," said Miss Watson with a frown. "Don't dare ask me how old I am. However, your question is important, so I will tell you I weigh 125 pounds. The older you are, the harder it is to keep your weight down."

"That's 325 pounds," replied Patrick. "Are you telling me the craft weighs only 75 pounds?"

"Oh, less than that," said Miss Watson. "We carry some equipment that weighs about 35 pounds."

"That leaves only 40 pounds," Patrick said in disbelief. "I can't believe this craft weighs 40 pounds."

"A little less," replied Miss Watson.

"How can that be?" asked Patrick.

"The craft is made of a special material that is strong and ultra-light," the principal answered. "The crew has to be able to lift it. We can't just leave a cloaked craft where people would bump into it. So, when we arrive for a mission we pick it up and put it somewhere safe, somewhere out of the way."

"So, you guys are both small to keep down the weight," asked Patrick. "Do they make you that way?"

"Oh, no," Miss Watson replied. "This is my natural size. I come from a family of small people. Only small people can time travel. So, your fellow students and most of your teachers will look like us."

"You'll love this," Mr. Smith said grinning. "Mapper teams wear green uniforms. When they were spotted, people thought they were aliens. That's where the idea of *little green men* came from. And, people decided time craft were from outer space, from other planets."

Mr. Smith took his head cover from the bench and pulled it over his head. "Does this look like anything you have seen before?" In place of his eyes were two large black oval lenses that allowed him to see when his head was covered.

"Yeah," Patrick replied. "You were wearing a full uniform when we saw you in the woods. That's why we didn't think you had mouths. You looked just like the drawings of aliens on TV and in magazines."

"It makes our job easier," added Miss Watson. "No one believes someone that says he saw little green men."

Patrick remembered Mike's father's reaction and nodded in agreement. "What about fuel? That must have a lot of weight?" he asked.

"There is no fuel, only power," Mr. Smith replied. "The craft is charged, like a battery. Charging a battery doesn't make it weigh more."

"I have to change the subject," Miss Watson said in a serious tone. "We have to talk about something important. You will become a pilot, Mr. Weaver. That means you are also the team leader. Mr. Pope and Mr. Castleton have jobs to do. They serve under you, but the mission is your job. That means everything is on your shoulders. Mr. Pope and Mr. Castleton have been your friends. Now, they are your crew, and they follow your orders. You are responsible for everything."

"You need to be a friend and a leader at the same time," Mr. Smith added. "That will change all three of you. You'll take a leadership class. It will help you a lot."

Mr. Smith looked at the control panel. "We're here," he told Patrick and Miss Watson.

Mike and Nick stood on the arrival/departure pad and watched Mr. Smith close the door. It reopened and there were Miss Watson and Patrick dressed in gray Fixer uniforms. "It's like a magic act," said Mike with a smile. "They're not there, and then they are."

"Hi guys. Been waiting long?" Patrick joked.

"We need to enroll you as cadets," said Mr. Smith. "Admissions is expecting you. It shouldn't take long, but we have to get there before they close. It's Friday afternoon."

"How did they know we were coming?" asked Mike.

"They knew we were bringing back a team," Miss Watson replied. "We told them to expect you three. If you had said no, it would have been someone else. Mr. Smith and I would have worked at Atlantic Academy until the right students attended, even if it took another 10 years. We have the time," she smiled.

"At admissions," continued Mr. Smith, "They'll give you your class schedules. You have four classes a day. You take your two morning classes together - *Ethics* and *History of Time Travel*. In the afternoon, you split up. Mr. Weaver, you'll be taking *Leadership Development* and *Crisis Management*. Mr. Pope you're studying *Time Craft Mechanics* and *Innovative Emergency Repairs*. Mr. Castleton, you get *Methods of Observation,* followed by *Practical Scientific Application.*

"Five weeks into the term, you'll begin your field training," Mr. Smith continued, stroking his thin mustache. "Mr. Weaver, you'll begin flight training and will learn to pilot a time craft. Mr. Pope, you'll be flying on missions and will repair the craft and equipment. Mr. Castleton, you will simulate missions and will practice observation and recording techniques."

Mike grimaced. His field training sounded boring. It looked like Patrick and Nick would have all the fun. Mr. Smith continued, "In a couple of months you will be briefed on the mission. At that time, we will tell you all we know about Dr. Morley's plans.

"After admissions, we'll check you into your dorm. Then, gentlemen we'll split up. One more point," Mr. Smith added. "You are in the future. You will find that we are polite and formal. It is easier to live in peace when everyone is respectful. That's why Miss Watson insists her students speak politely. First, it makes the past more comfortable for us. Second, you don't have to adapt to the future. We've already prepared you to live here."

The boys enrolled as Time Institute cadets. Admissions gave them ID cards to wear around their necks. They got their class schedules and a campus map. They were also assigned a dorm room.

They were told to wear their uniforms at all times, as that identified them. They only had one uniform, but the cloth was self-cleaning. Laundry was a thing of the past. Mr. Smith explained that this was another old technology. Scientists were working on self-cleaning fabrics during the boys' time.

Mike thought of all the times his mother had scolded him for not changing his clothes. "In the future, I'm right and she's wrong," he laughed.

"Mr. Smith?" Nick asked. "How long will we be here?"

"The term is seven months," the Social Studies teacher answered. "You get several one week breaks."

"We'll grow and change in that amount of time," Mike explained. "When we get back, won't our parents notice? We won't look like we did when they dropped us off this morning?"

"No," replied Mr. Smith. "You'll be exactly the same. It's a strange thing. We only grow older in our own time. When we leave, we stop aging. Even our fingernails and hair don't grow. In fact, you won't need to eat or drink, unless you choose to. The same happens to Miss Watson and me when we're at Atlantic Academy. It's a phenomenon called the experience of time. You're now outside time. You'll experience time as if it's passing, but for you, it's not. You'll see the hands on the clock move. The sun sets and rises. You'll get tired. But, you won't get older. You'll return to your time exactly the same age you are now."

"So, I was right," Mike said. "I was thinking a while ago. All the years I've been at Atlantic Academy Miss Watson never grew older."

"Careful," warned Mr. Smith with a smile and a wink at the principal. "Miss Watson does not like people to talk about her age."

Patrick turned to Mike and said, "Two things you never ask a woman, her weight and her age." Mike and Nick wondered where he had picked up this strange wisdom.

"The experience of time has its advantages," Mr. Smith continued. "A time traveler can get up in the morning and work ten years in the past. He'll go home that night and have supper with his family, not a day older. It's as I warned you; time travel messes with your mind."

Dr. Smith became serious. "But. There is a *but* to the experience of time, and it's a big but. You don't age, *but* you are not immortal. You can be killed in another time. Time travelers have died on missions. We lost some good friends a while ago in an accident at Roswell, New Mexico."

Chapter 12

The Time Institute

"Dorm rooms haven't changed," said Nick. "This is like the one at hockey camp."

"Space Camp dorms look like the inside of a space ship," Mike commented.

"You guys had it easy," Patrick grumbled as he took the towels off his bed and put them on his bureau. "At Ti Kwon Do Camp we slept in tents on the ground. They said it was to toughen us up. In comparison, this is like staying at the Sheraton."

The boys set up their dorm room and then walked down to the cafeteria on the first floor. They ate supper, and then went to bed. Mike looked at the clock on the wall. It was nearly 8:00 and the sun was just setting. He thought it must be late summer. Realizing he didn't know the date recalled what Mr. Smith had said. Time travel messes with your mind. Nick put his head on the pillow and started to snore. He always went to bed at 8:00 as his hockey games were scheduled early in the morning. "Patrick?" Mike whispered to his other friend. There was no answer. Mike thought about the past couple of days as he too, drifted off.

Mike's eyes popped open. The sun was up and light was pouring into the dorm room. He looked at the clock to discover it was already 7:30. He rolled out from under the covers and sat on the edge of the bed. He glanced at Patrick's bunk and saw the back of his friend's head on the pillow. The rest of him was under a blanket.

He looked at Nick's bed. It was made, but Nick was not there and his Fixer uniform was missing. Mike knew he had gotten up early and left. It was no surprise. All those morning hockey games had trained Nick to wake at 5:00.

"Patrick," Mike called gently. His friend moaned. "Patrick, it's time to get up. Nick's already gone." Mike was dressed and making his own bed when Nick returned. Patrick was just getting out of the shower.

"Where did you go?" asked Mike.

"Exploring," Nick answered. "I found the subway station and read the map, so I know how to get where we have to go. By the way," he added. "These uniforms really do clean themselves. Last night at supper I spilled some mustard and ketchup on myself. This morning the stain is gone. The uniform looks brand new."

"Cool," said Mike.

Patrick dressed and they went down for breakfast. "I figure we have three things to do," Mike said between bites of food. "We should get our books and supplies at the bookstore. We should find our way to the MacDonald Center and locate our classrooms. We don't want to be looking for them Monday morning. Then, we should do some sightseeing."

"No," Nick responded. "I think we should start with the sightseeing. If we go to the bookstore first, we'll be carrying our books around with us all day."

"You want to get the important stuff done first. You want to be sure you have enough time," Mike insisted.

"Hauling all that stuff around doesn't make any sense," Nick shot back.

"Gentlemen," said Patrick holding up his hands.

"Gentlemen?" asked Nick with surprise. "You sound like Mr. Smith."

"Yes," Patrick replied. "But it works. You both stopped talking. Look Nick, Mike is right. First, we do the things we have to do and get them out of the way. Mike, Nick is right too. We don't want to be carrying our books around with us all day. So, here's the plan. We'll start out at the MacDonald Center and find our classrooms while our arms are still empty. Then, we'll go to the bookstore. After, we'll return here and drop off our books in our room. Finally, we'll go see UNH. It's Saturday. We can be out as late as we want."

Mike and Nick looked at Patrick with amazement. "Ay, Ay, Sir," said Nick. Patrick felt something new. He was in command. He had made the decision and the other two had accepted his leadership without question.

The boys arrived at the MacDonald Center. Inside the entrance they found a diagram on the wall that showed how to get around the building. "How do we figure this out?" Patrick asked.

"It's called a floor plan," said Nick, looking at his course schedule. "*Ethics* is in Room 203. We walk down this corridor," he explained, showing Mike and Patrick the corridor on the floor plan. "There will be a staircase on the right. At the top we are only one door away. *History of Time Travel* is in Room 107. We go back down the same stairs and turn right. The classroom should be three doors down."

"How did you figure this out?" Mike asked.

"Easy," Nick answered. "I had to read lots of diagrams this summer when I was working with my Grandpa on that sports car. Once you learn, all diagrams are pretty easy."

Mike and Patrick looked at the floor plan and were glad it was easy for Nick, because it wasn't for them. "Take us to the bookstore," Patrick said to Nick.

Admissions had told the boys the custom of touching Dr. MacDonald's plaque when entering or exiting the MacDonald Center. Before they left each put a finger on the shiny spot. They also paused to read the plaque. "If we fail," said Patrick "This building will never be built. I'm not sure what Mr. Smith meant when he said Morley would cause Chaos, but it sure sounded bad. Gentlemen, failure is not an option. This job is too important. It scares me, but we have to pull it off."

The boys walked to the bus stop in a serious mood. Right now, they were on an adventure, but they knew this adventure would end. When it did, it turned into a critical mission when everything would depend on them.

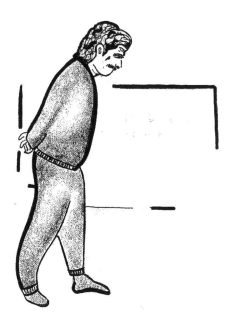

Chapter 13

Second First Day of School

Patrick led Nick and Mike into room 203 of the MacDonald Center for their first class. They were a bit early and there was no one else in the room. They sat at desks near the front. "This is our second first day of school this year," Mike joked.

The other cadets began to trickle in. They were no taller than the boys. In fact, they were so consistently the same small size, the casual observer would have guessed the Institute was a school for gymnasts. While the same height and weight as the three twelve -year olds, their fellows were a bit older. Mike guessed that back home they would be in the Atlantic Academy High School. The cadets came from all over the world. Everyone spoke English, but often with a bit of an accent. Their uniforms were either red Researchers or green Mappers. There weren't any other gray Fixer uniforms.

At 8:30 the teacher entered. He walked to his desk at the front of the room and placed some books and papers on it. As he looked up at the cadet faces he became serious. "My name is Dr. Charles Newcomb," he said. "This is the most important class you will take at the Time Institute. Our ethics code controls all your actions as time travelers. Whether you are trained as pilots, science observers, or engineers, you must always conduct yourselves the way I teach you. Whether you join a Research team, a Mapper team, or …," Dr. Newcomb hesitated and stared at the boys with a puzzled expression. A look of understanding and recognition came over his face and he nodded to the three. "Or, a Fixer team," he added. "Ethics guides all our time travels.

"You cannot join a time team without earning at least a B in this class. Anything less is considered a failing grade. You will not be allowed into a time craft unless you take an oath to always follow our code of ethics." Dr. Newcomb placed his hands behind his back and began to pace back and forth in front of his desk, looking at the floor as he walked. His face relaxed to its normal smiling expression as he gave his students time to ponder what he had just said.

"Why are our ethics so important?" he asked, not expecting an answer. "As cadets you will hear often a quote from my father. He was a Fixer pilot during the Institute's early years. He said, 'Time travel messes with your mind.' Why did he say that? On missions, things happen that confuse you, and make you wonder what is real. People that do a lot of traveling sometimes wake up not knowing where they are. That happens to time travelers too, but they also wake up not knowing *when* they are.

Because of the experience of time you can live years in the past. You begin to think that is where you belong. When the mission ends, you wake up in your own bed the day you left. You're not sure if the mission was real, or a dream.

"It's possible to see people in the past that you know in the present. It's possible to run into yourself in the past. If we can access the past, is it really past? What makes it different from the present? You are training as time crews. That means the past is in your future.

"Human history is horrible. You'll see things so awful you want to stop them. Stopping them will seem like the right thing to do. It will be the wrong thing. You can't interfere. You'll feel guilty and confused. You'll have nightmares about the things you've witnessed."

Dr. Newcomb continued pacing, looking at the floor ahead of his feet. "We have our ethics code because we are human, and all people are tied together by our common humanity. Your humanity ties you to everyone living now, or who has ever lived. A caveman living in a cave is as human as you. A nomad living in the open desert is as human as you. A Native American living in a wigwam is no different from anyone in this room. An Inuit living in an igloo is the same as you in every way."

Dr. Newcomb paused again. "You must never think you are better than any other human being. This is the most important thing I will tell you this term. Whenever you deal with people in the past, treat them with care and respect. Treat them with the same care and respect you would want for yourself, and for the people you love. You would not want a time traveler to terrify your mother. So, you must be careful to never scare or hurt anyone in the past. Everything else I teach you will be based on this."

Nick, Patrick, and Mike didn't have to imagine being scared. They remembered seeing the two time crews in the woods and what it had done to them.

"This is the second thing you have to learn," Dr. Newcomb continued. He became serious again, and again his smile disappeared. "All human beings have a right to their own time. They have a right to their experiences, just as much as you do. Whether their lives are happy or miserable, those are their lives, and they are sacred. You must treat their time and their experiences with the same care and respect you would want for yours. It is wrong to cause Chaos for another person by changing their history. You cannot do it, even if you think you are helping them. All your actions must be carried out with care and caution and complete adherence to our code of ethics."

Dr. Newcomb paused. "In a perfect world, we would not need Fixer teams," he said looking at the three boys. "You must be sure," he said to the whole class, "they have as little work as possible.

"You studied world history in the schools that sent you here. You know that in the past, stronger peoples controlled weaker peoples." Dr. Newcomb paused again as he walked back and forth behind his desk with his hands clasped behind him. This was how he taught. He said something important and then paused and paced. His pauses gave students time to think. "Those stronger peoples – the ones that controlled and killed weaker peoples - they were no different from you." He slowly moved his finger around the room pointing at the students. "And they were no different from me." His smile disappeared again as he pointed at himself.

"We have learned to keep pride, greed, and envy under control. Never forget, we only keep them under control. As I said, we share our humanity with all people. We share the same rights, but we also share the same nature. If you take away our technology and training, we are the same as history's stronger peoples. This is why this class is so important," continued Dr. Newcomb. "We can never let ourselves slip. We can never revert to our common nature. This class will teach you to always respect other people. It will teach you to treat them with the same care you would want for yourself."

Dr. Newcomb ended his opening lecture and devoted the rest of the class time to discussion. Dr. Newcomb would think up a situation, and then asked students what they would do in that case. It was a fun way to pass time. It made everyone think and participate.

At the end of class the students filed out. As the boys passed by, Dr. Newcomb called them to his desk. "Fixer uniforms," he said smiling. "Fixers always have lots of missions under their belts. They usually have some gray hair and a few wrinkles. I've never seen young Fixers before." Again, one of his pauses and a smile. "I'm guessing you were brought here for a very specific mission. Right?"

The boys did not know how to respond. Back at Atlantic Academy Mr. Smith had told them to not talk to anyone about the mission. Patrick spoke for the group. "Sir, we don't know who we can talk with and what we can say."

"Excellent answer," Dr. Newcomb replied, his smile even broader. "Don't tell me anything. Just listen. I chair the committee dealing with the Dr. Morley matter. I know everything and I will be there when you are briefed on the mission. Meanwhile, give your teachers your best effort. We will send you off as prepared as possible."

Mike asked, "Dr. Newcomb, is Charles a family name?"

"Yes, it is," Dr. Newcomb replied with a bit of surprise. "Every generation of my family has had a Charles."

"Did they all live in this area?" asked Mike.

"The first Charles came to New Hampshire from Baltimore, a little before your time. He came here to teach music. He was the only Newcomb newcomer," the teacher said, smiling at the pun he had made of his family's name. "Otherwise, we have always lived here. Why do you ask?"

"I think we know him," answered Mike. "He's a really nice guy and a good teacher too."

"I'm proud to know that," said Dr. Newcomb with a nod, a smile, and a slight bow. "Now, off to your next class."

As the boys exited the classroom Mike said to his friends, "Just think, our Ethics teacher is our Music teacher's great-great-something grandson. Time travel does mess with your mind."

Chapter 14
History of Time Travel

Every cadet took *History of Time Travel,* so the class of cadets moved as a group to Room 107. The teacher's name was Rabbi Jacob Cohen and he was already in the classroom waiting for the cadets.

Rabbi Cohen's teaching style was different from Dr. Newcomb's. Dr. Newcomb said important things and then paused to give the students time to think. Meanwhile, he walked back and forth with his hands behind his back, looking at the floor. Rabbi Cohen was much livelier. He got excited. He waved his hands. He laughed at his own jokes.

Rabbi Cohen was also surprised to see three boys in Fixer uniforms. He quickly realized who they were and nodded to them as Dr. Newcomb had done.

"Shalom. Welcome to *History of Time Travel*," he said to the class. "A great thinker once said, people who do not know history are doomed to repeat it. You all took *World History* courses in the schools that sent you here. So, you all know that history is full of terrible things we do not want to repeat. Since we started to time travel crews have made mistakes. We don't want to repeat those either. Our goal is to get better at our work and create fewer problems. Maybe someday, we will not need Fixer Teams." He nodded again to Patrick, Nick, and Mike.

"What better place to start a history class than at the beginning?" he asked with a chuckle at his own joke. A holographic image of a caveman dressed in animal skins appeared in front of the class. The caveman was staring up at the sky. He seemed so real the boys were sure they could touch him.

"Early humans like this fellow here, started the problem of misunderstanding time," Rabbi Cohen said. "He watched the sun rise in the morning and set in the evening. He called the light *day* and the dark *night*. Every night, he watched the moon grow bigger or smaller. It went from a full moon to a tiny sliver.

Then, it became full again. He counted how many nights the moon took to do this. There were always 28. He named these 28 nights a month – *a moonth*. He laughed as his joke.

"The calendar was the next problem with understanding time." The holographic image changed and three men appeared. They were dressed in cloth and leather and were working to lift a huge rectangular stone. "These men are working on Stonehenge. It is a prehistoric circle of upright stones in England. People who planted crops needed to know when spring would arrive. So they built large sun calendars like this one. I don't know how they turned the pages." He laughed again.

Another holographic figure appeared in front of the class. This man was sitting at a bench and working with little wheels and gears. The boys realized he was making a clock. "With clocks, people thought they were learning to understand time better. The opposite was happening," Rabbi Cohen said.

"Human beings misunderstood time for so many centuries that we need to talk about what time is really like. Have you ever seen an old movie?" the teacher asked. He held up a strip of motion picture film. "When movies were first invented they were made on this stuff." He stretched the strip of film between his hands so the class could see it better. "Movie film is a long series of frames. It was made by a special camera that opened and closed over and over at a certain speed. Each time the shutter opened, light hit the film and made a picture that caught the action at that moment. Like this one here," he said pointing to a single frame. "The next frame occurs just after the first, and so on. When frames were played back on a projector, the audience saw the action on a screen."

Rabbi Cohen picked up a pair of scissors. "If you took all the little pictures and cut them into individual frames, you could stack them like you would stack a deck of cards." He began to cut the film and pile the frames one on top of the next. "They are still in the same order as when they were a roll of film. However, instead of being in a strip, each frame now stands alone."

He picked up the stack of film between his fingers and showed it to the class. "This stack is what time is like. We call the stack a sequence." Rabbi Cohen paused and smiled. "No matter how long the sequence, every frame in it exists. To go to a specific event a time traveler only needs to know the sequence and where the frame is. Then, just like in this stack, it is possible to arrive at that moment. Understand?" The class all nodded. "Those of you who are training as

Mappers, this is the work you do. You identify and map sequences and frames. It is a huge job, so big we don't know if it will ever be finished." Again, Rabbi Cohen paused to let the class think about the scale of the mapping project. "Mappers have job security," he added, laughing at the joke.

"The way you talk is strange to us," said Mike. "You don't talk about when things happened. You don't use dates, or hours, and years. It's all frames and sequences. It's hard to understand. Do we have to learn to talk like this?"

Rabbi Cohen responded, "We have to be places on time. So yes, we do use minutes, hours, and days. However, there is a reality. Reality is that time, the fourth dimension, is made up of frames and sequences.

"Let's get back to the sequences," he said. "You can't see them, so I will give you an idea of what they are like." Another holographic image appeared. This one showed long rows of regularly spaced dominos standing on end. The rows twisted and curved and crisscrossed each other over and over, forming a complex web. "Time sequences are like these dominos," Rabbi Cohen explained. "Think of each row as a sequence and each domino as a frame. Every time I meet someone, our sequences, our rows, crisscross. Think of all the people who have ever lived and you can understand that all these sequences make a huge and complex web.

"Look again at the holograph," Rabbi Cohen told the class. "If the end domino is knocked over, you know all the dominos ahead of it will fall." The class waited to see if that would happen. It would be fun to watch.

"This is how History of Time Travel fits together with your Ethics class," Rabbi Cohen explained. He pointed at the image and an unseen finger pushed the first domino. The rows began to fall. The falling dominos in one row crisscrossed other rows. All those rows began to fall, as well. These reached other rows and started those falling. It looked like a big wave was moving across the image.

Rabbi Cohen became very serious and paused as he looked at the room full of cadets. "The same happens when time is altered," he warned. "If a frame is changed it acts like one of those dominos. This is what we mean by the term *Chaos*. Changing a frame sets off Chaos through all the following frames. Think of each row of dominos as a person's life. Knock over one frame in one row and you change everything else. You create Chaos in that person's sequence. That

Chaos passes on to other people, spreading out like the dominos."

The stunned class stared at the fallen dominos, every cadet deep in thought. Until now, time travel had seemed exciting. They had just learned that they were taking on an enormous responsibility. If they were careless they could ruin countless lives. After a while Rabbi Cohen added, "That's why we have Fixer teams. They stop changes before they set off Chaos. Do not ask them to fix your mistakes. It is better not to make mistakes in the first place. You won't, if you follow the rules Dr. Newcomb is teaching you.

"Let's get back to our subject. The history of time travel begins at the Hampton Summit." A holographic image of Dr. MacDonald appeared in front of the class. He appeared to be working and talking to someone. Miss Watson had told the boys about Dr. MacDonald, but they had not seen him. They hadn't known he was disabled and got around in an electric wheelchair.

"The world after the Hampton Summit was exciting," Rabbi Cohen continued. "Two important things happened that you will be studying in this class. First, our scientists built spaceships with fast ion engines. This allowed us to explore the solar system and the space around it." Mike and his friends perked up at the mention of space travel.

"Second, other scientists studied the fourth dimension – time. They learned to understand frames and sequences, but they could not use them. That requires a huge amount of power, more power than we could create. So, time travel remained only a theory.

"It stayed a theory until, just beyond the planet Pluto, a space crew discovered one end of a wormhole." A holographic image of the wormhole appeared. It was a long curved tunnel, like a tornado in space. "We sent probes into the wormhole. They found a black hole near the other end." The image changed to show the black hole. It swirled like a glowing whirlpool of stars with a large black patch in the center.

"We sent a crew into the wormhole to visit the black hole," Rabbi Cohen continued. "A black hole is a source of enormous power. Does anyone know where it gets all that power?"

"Yes, Sir," Mike responded. Rabbi Cohen gestured to him. "Black holes are caused by collapsed dead stars," Mike explained. "Gravity squeezes their matter into a point the size of a single atom called a singularity. A black hole's gravity is so strong even light isn't fast enough to get out. That's why the center of the holographic image is black."

Rabbi Cohen nodded. He had been surprised by this detailed explanation. "Do you know what escape velocity is?" he asked the cadet, with a hint of hesitation.

"Yes, Sir," Mike continued. "Escape velocity is the speed needed to break free of a planet's gravity. To break free from earth a rocket has to go 25,000 miles per hour. Light speed is the fastest speed possible. So, if a black hole's escape velocity is greater than the speed of light, you can imagine how powerful its gravitational pull must be." Mike paused and thought about what he just said. "No," he corrected himself. "We can't imagine how powerful a black hole is. It's beyond our understanding."

The surprised class of cadets all stared at Mike. "How do you know all this?" Rabbi Cohen asked.

"My father keeps giving me all these science magazines to read. I've been to Space Camp twice, and I study all the time to become an astronaut."

"I'm not sure what any of that means," replied Rabbi Cohen with a puzzled look. "But it obviously pays off. Anyway, back to our story. We had found a source for the power needed to time travel. We built a power plant at the black hole." An image of the factory appeared.

"Why isn't the power plant sucked into the black hole along with everything else?" asked Nick.

"Good question, Mr. Fixer," said Rabbi Cohen. "We reversed the power plant's polarity so it is the opposite of the black hole's gravity. Then we adjusted the push and pull until they were in equilibrium, perfectly balancing each other. That means the power plant pushes away from the black hole with the same amount of force that pulls it in. You may have felt a similar force playing with magnets. That's why the factory stays where it is.

"There was still one very big problem. It is a long trip from here to there. Going to the worm hole and getting back took far too long. It was impractical." Rabbi Cohen began to speak slowly, his way of telling the class to listen carefully. "This led to another exciting discovery. You know that a black hole's gravity creates an escape velocity faster than the speed of light. What happens if you reverse its polarity? If you make the force push away, rather than pull in?"

Mike stared at Rabbi Cohen as he worked out the answer in his mind. His eyes slowly widened into saucers. The answer was beyond belief. "That's not possible. The pushing force would be greater the speed of light!" he blurted.

"It is possible," said Rabbi Cohen full of excitement. "The pushing force is faster than the speed of light. We had found a way to propel our craft. Now, we had everything. We already knew about sequences and frames. The black hole gave us the power we needed to access them. It also gave us hyper-light speed so we could go back and forth quickly. Time travel was no longer a dream. It became real." Rabbi Cohen was very proud of all this achievement and he took a moment to enjoy the satisfaction.

"In future lessons you will study about time travel's early years. You will read how the Time Institute became part of UNH. You will learn how the different time teams were created and what they do. You will learn about Mapper teams mapping the sequences. You will read about Researcher teams and how they help historians and scholars. Tonight, read chapters one through three in your text book. I'll see you tomorrow."

Chapter 15
Allie

After history class the boys walked to the
cafeteria for lunch. They ate and then split up, each
going to his afternoon classes. Patrick went to
Leadership Development where he learned how to
handle responsibility. He had already taken over as
team leader. He was happy Nick and Mike accepted
his new role and did not give him a hard time. It was
Patrick's nature to take a job seriously. He did not

want to be team leader, but he was. This mission was critical and he was determined to do it right.

Full of excitement, Nick took off for his class in *Time Craft Mechanics.* He could hardly wait to see inside these craft and learn how they worked. Mike's next class was *Methods of Observation.* It sounded dull, so he didn't share his friends' enthusiasm.

After these classes, the boys met again in the hallway. Patrick's and Nick's last classes of the day – *Crisis Management* and *Innovative Emergency Repairs* - began in 15 minutes. Mike's last class – *Practical Scientific Application* – was not until the period after that. Since Mike had nothing to do for the next hour, he decided to go back to the cafeteria. He would use his free time to start his homework.

"Let's all meet back at the dorm after school," Patrick suggested. "We can have supper together and then go back to our room to study." The other two agreed with the plan, and they split up again. Nick climbed the stairs to his classroom as Patrick started down the corridor towards his. Mike turned and walked back to the cafeteria. He found a small table and opened his *Ethics* text book. He began to read about people who had accidentally seen time travelers. The shock had caused mental problems for some of them. Others were even frightened to death. Mike understood how this could happen. He remembered how he and his friends had reacted to seeing time crews in the woods.

Mike was so busy reading he did not notice a small girl approach his table. "Excuse me," said the girl. Mike was startled and bumped the table, causing his text book to fall to the floor. "I'm so sorry," the girl apologized as Mike leaned down to pick up his book. The girl steadied the table so nothing else would go flying. "I didn't mean to startle you," the girl said. She spoke with a slight accent that told Mike she had not grown up speaking English.

Mike looked up at the girl and his jaw dropped. She had long, straight auburn hair that reached below her shoulders and flipped under at the ends. Her eyes were deep brown and her skin was the color of cream. Even though she had red hair she had no freckles, just a touch of rose on her smooth cheeks, like on a peach. To be polite, Mike stood up, but once again he bumped the table. Again, the girl steadied it. Mike tried to say something, but only croaked like a frog. He couldn't stop his mind from repeating over and over, "She is so beautiful. She is so beautiful." He finally managed to ask the girl if she wanted to sit. She accepted.

"I'm really sorry I frightened you," the girl said. Mike's mind raced as he stared at her, trying to think of something intelligent to say. The girl was a little older than he and was wearing a red Researcher uniform. "My name is Aleksandra Tymoshenko," the girl said, offering her hand to the flustered boy. "My friends call me Allie." Mike knew she was inviting him to be her friend and shook her hand.

"I'm Mike," the boy answered, grateful that his throat had begun to work again. "Where do you come from Allie?"

"I grew up in Ukraine," she explained. "It's a large country in Central Europe. My family is still there."

She changed the subject. "You're one of the boys from the past?" She asked it as a question, but said it as a fact. This caught Mike by surprise. He had been told twice not to not talk about his mission, once by Mr. Smith, and then by Dr. Newcomb. He hesitated. "Don't worry," Allie reassured him. "Everyone knows you are here at The Institute. A thing like that gets around real fast. The rest of us don't know why you are here, and we've been told not to ask. So, I won't. But I do know who you are."

Mike wanted this girl to stay and searched for a way to make that happen. "Would you like something to drink?" he asked. She smiled and nodded. The two got up from their chairs and walked to the counter together. All the way, Mike's mind was stuck on one thought. *She is so pretty.*

"I'm a music history student," Allie explained. "I'm training to serve on a Researcher team. I'll be a science observer studying music in the past." Mike nodded. This was good. She was training for the same job he was, and she studied music. They already had two things in common, two things he could talk about without making a fool of himself.

"Do you like music?" Allie asked.

Mike nodded his head enthusiastically. "I play electric guitar," he replied, happy to have managed something that did not sound stupid.

"That's great," said the redheaded girl with a smile, causing Mike's heart to race and skip beats. Suddenly, he realized he was not breathing. He felt faint. He forced his body to take a deep breath.

"Do you know anything about music history?" Allie asked. Perhaps it was her friendly manner. Or, perhaps the deep breathing, but Mike was beginning to feel better. Yes, he knew a lot about this subject. Allie placed her elbows on the table and rested her chin on her folded hands. This brought her much closer to Mike. He thought she smelled good, like soap.

"Yeah," he said. "I study music all the time. It's a major thing for me. I like 20th century popular music, beginning with Ragtime." Allie's eyes widened. It seemed she liked what she heard and was inviting Mike to keep talking.

"I listen to a lot of Big Band. I think the best music ever was from the 1930s and 1940s. I love Glenn Miller and Benny Goodman. I like Frank Sinatra, Gene Kelly, and Fred Astaire as singers."

"How about the later decades?" Allie asked. Mike guessed she had her own opinions. Had she asked that question to see if he agreed? How should he respond? He didn't want to turn her off. He decided he should give an honest answer and hope for the best.

"The 1950s were pretty good," he began. "Buddy Holly was great. He opened the door for guys like Chuck Berry and Elvis. They created Rock and Roll. By 1960 rock groups had lost their way and recorded a lot of really lame songs. Some Doo Wop was pretty good, though. It had lots of nice vocal harmonies."

Allie continued to look at Mike with her chin on her hands. Her eyes were locked on his and they remained wide open. He liked having her stare at him with so much interest. He figured she liked what she heard and continued, "The 1960s started out really bad. A lot of British Invasion groups weren't very good. The Beatles, they were innovative. Because of them, other groups started to experiment and tried to create their own sound. Nobody wanted to sound like anyone else. Some really good stuff was recorded."

Allie continued to listen. She even nodded from time to time. Mike was on a roll. "The 1970s created the best Rock and Roll. Groups like AC/DC, Led Zeppelin, and Queen wrote songs that were truly great. The music mattered to them. They focused on their sound. Angus Young from AC/DC was the greatest guitarist ever. I copy him a lot."

Allie smiled at that personal note. "After that, groups relied on gimmicks. They wore high platform shoes and put on crazy make up. They smashed their guitars, or set them on fire. The music wasn't important any more. They just wanted to shock the audience.

"The 1980s and 1990s were awful," Mike added. Singers performed dance routines while they sang. They added displays of flashing lights and fireworks. The dancing and the visuals were all that mattered. The music was really lame. It's still that way. And to make it worse, they fix the music with computers. If a singer or a musician isn't all that good, the studio fixes their music so they sound right, so they sound better than they really are. There's not much real music right now," Mike said. By *right now,* he meant his own time.

"That's what my teacher said last year in my *History of Popular Music* class," Allie replied, her chin still on her hands, still leaning in towards Mike. "Just like you, he said the end of the 20th century was all gimmicks. He said music stayed like that for a long time. Then, the Sirens changed everything. They were so daring they set off a whole new wave of creativity. He used a word to describe the Sirens and their music. He said they were *audacious.*" At hearing his band's name Mike's eyes widened in surprise. Allie noticed. "Do you know the Sirens?" she asked. "I thought they were a bit later than your time."

"I've heard of them," Mike answered with hesitation. "They're around, but they're not really well known yet."

"This is awesome!" Allie replied with delight. "You know about the Sirens' early years? No one knows for sure how they developed their sound. It was called Chamber Rock. It was performed in small rooms for small audiences, instead of in big theaters and arenas. The Sirens were so popular all the other groups copied them and started playing Chamber Rock. It was the most exciting sound in music for years. I became so interested in the band that I wrote my research paper about them.

"One day, the Sirens just stopped playing. No one knows why," she added with a combination of curiosity and disappointment in her voice. "It's surprising that so little information remains about a group as famous and influential as the Sirens. It made it difficult to do that paper. The 21st century kept records of everyone else, but not about the Sirens. We know they played that last major event and just disappeared. We don't even know what happened to the band members." She paused for a moment and then continued. "So, you have listened to the Sirens in their early years. This is gold for a music historian," she said with excitement.

Mike was nervous. He didn't want to get into any time problems like the Grandfather Paradox. He decided not to tell Allie that he was the Sirens' lead guitarist and song writer. On second thought, he couldn't see how that could change the future. He became confused, so he glanced at the clock. "Oh, look," he said. "I have my last class in ten minutes. I'd better get up to my classroom."

"I'll go with you," offered Allie. "We can sit together." Mike looked puzzled. "I'm training as a science observer too," she explained. "We're taking the same classes. You didn't see me before because you always sit up front. I was behind you."

Mike liked this. Allie was in all his classes. She really liked music. He really liked her, and she seemed to like him. After all, she did suggest they sit together in class. The pair got up from the table. Mike picked up their glasses and brought them to the kitchen window.

"How old are you Allie?" Mike asked.

"It's not polite to ask a woman her age," Allie said with a smile. Mike remembered Patrick saying that and wondered why it was such a big secret. He knew his mother's age, and she was a woman. Allie grinned. "I finished early at my sending school. I'm younger than most of the other cadets. I may be bit older than you, but don't let that bother you. I think you are very grown up. And you're very interesting."

After class Allie and Mike left the classroom together. "I promised to have supper with my roommates," Mike said. "Then, we're doing homework. But I really hope you and I can study together a lot," he added.

"I'd like to do that," Allie responded. She held her books in front of her, smiling at Mike with both her mouth and her eyes. "How about we start tomorrow?"

"Yeah," Mike said enthusiastically. "That'll be great. I'll see you in class in the morning. Don't sit in the back. Sit with me, and Patrick and Nick. You'll like them," he said with confidence.

Allie turned to go and then stopped. "Mike," she said. "I don't even know your last name."

"It's uh, uh, Castleton," Mike answered with hesitation. It was Allie's turn to be surprised. Her eyes opened wide as she realized who he was.

"Oh, no. This can't be. You're Captain Mike, Mike Castleton of the Sirens? This can't be true."

"It's true," Mike admitted quietly, almost timidly.

"Nick? Patrick? Those other boys in class. They're Nick Pope and Patrick Weaver, aren't they? It really is you. I can't believe it." Mike just nodded, unable to add anything. Allie had figured it out all by herself. "Where are the others?" Allie asked abruptly.

"Others?" Mike answered with surprise.

"Yes, the other band members. Where are they?"

"What do you mean?" Mike responded with puzzlement. "There are just the three of us."

"You mean you didn't all start out all together?" Allie said in wonderment at such an important revelation. Suddenly, she realized she had blundered into a forbidden conversation. "Don't tell anyone I talked about the Sirens," she said seriously. "That's stuff you shouldn't know. After all, that is your future, your sequence, your frames. I don't want to change anything." She paused a moment. "You know I can't tell you anything more," she said. "It wouldn't be right." Mike nodded in understanding.

"I'll be watching you very carefully, Captain Mike," Allie added with a sly smile. "I can't believe I know you and Nick and Patrick before you started Chamber Rock. I know I can't ask you about your early music. But maybe I'll discover that special thing you guys have, that thing that caused a revolution in music. I'll find where that legendary audacity comes from. This is a music historian's dream come true."

"I hope you'll like me for who I am, not who I become," said Mike sheepishly.

"Oh, I like you a lot, just the way you are Mike," Allie replied. "I liked you a whole lot before I learned your last name. I wanted to see you a whole lot too."

Allie turned and walked down the corridor. Mike followed her with his eyes. He thought how nice it was to watch her long, shiny auburn hair sway side-to-side with each step. Then, he turned and headed off to the dorm.

Chapter 16

Morley and His Minions

Dr. Roger Morley stood upright between the two benches in a time craft cabin. He had his hands on his hips with his elbows stuck out to the side. He turned his head to the right, bent his neck so he was looking slightly upward, and jutted his jaw forward. He held the pose a moment. Next, he folded his arms across his chest, lowered his face, and looked out under his eye brows with a determined stare.

Being a time traveler and a Researcher S/O Dr. Morley was small, no bigger than Dr. Newcomb or Rabbi Cohen. He had a hooked nose, so hooked it almost formed a quarter circle. He wore a goatee that was streaked with white. His eyebrows were so thick and bushy they ran together into one heavy line above his eyes. Dr. Morley was older than Dr. Newcomb and Rabbi Cohen and his face was sallow with lots of wrinkles. However, his hair was dark brown. This was curious, as his goatee was streaked with white and his single eyebrow was gray.

Two men in purple uniforms stood at the front of the craft with their backs facing Dr. Morley. The two men were the same height as the older man, but far stronger. Their broad shoulders stretched their uniforms tight, and their large upper arms did the same. Their thick necks were as wide as their heads. The man on the left was Collin Teller. He was piloting the craft, while the other, Lars Bryant, helped him. Bryant turned and with curiosity watched Dr. Morley posing. "What are you doing, Excellency?" he asked.

"I am practicing the poses I will use when addressing my people, and when I am being photographed for official portraits," Morley answered. "Every dictator had a favorite pose that displayed authority and power. I am imitating dictators from the past to find the pose that works best for me. People must recognize me as being in charge. People naturally follow the strong, and so I must look strong. We will have less trouble with them if they accept me as their emperor. It will be easier than always forcing them to obey my will."

"Is that why you dyed your hair?" Teller asked.

"Yes," Dr. Morley answered. "I want to look younger and more vigorous. I think I can cover my wrinkles with makeup," he muttered to himself.

Rather than giggle at their leader's vanity the two men watched him in awe. They were convinced the older man had everything planned and well-thought out. They were confident they would soon have important jobs in his world-wide government.

"Dictators always wore military uniforms," Morley said, changing his train of thought. "This one will do fine," he concluded, looking down at his red Researcher uniform. Time Institute uniforms look like sweat suits, hardly the crisp, tailored uniforms worn by dictators. "I will have to add some medals to my chest and some insignia," he mused. "And I should sew on some gold braid, and I should wear a sash, a gold sash. That would look good too.

"I need an appropriate title," Morley said, abruptly changing his line of thought again. His fevered mind did this frequently. His minions turned and looked at him quizzically as he explained, "Every dictator in history used the word *Leader*. In other languages the titles *El Caudillo, Der Fuehrer, Il Duce*, all mean Leader. That title is worn out. I need to find something more impressive. "I'm thinking of something like Eternal Guide. The first word reminds people I am divine. The second sends the message I am helping my people out of love and duty, rather than forcing them. People don't like to be forced. A good dictator fools people into thinking *they* are in charge, going where *they* want. He fools them into thinking he serves them. They are all sheep and don't know the difference. They will happily follow Morleyism."

"Morleyism?" Bryant asked. "That sounds like something people believe."

"It is," Morley explained as he smoothed out his red uniform. "Morelyism is my philosophy. It is the philosophy of the Eternal Guide, Morley the Great."

"What is your teaching, Excellency?" Teller asked.

"That I am all that matters," Morley announced. "Nothing else in the world matters. That is Morleyism. It is a very simple philosophy." The two minions nodded like some deep and secret knowledge had just been revealed to them.

Morley arched his arms over his head and touched his fingertips together. "Do this," he told his minions. It was like he was playing Simon Says, or like he was leading a class of kindergartners in a silly song. The two minions mimicked the Eternal Guide's pose. "I like that," Morley announced with satisfaction. "That will be our official salute. In this position our arms form a circle. A circle has no beginning or end, just like me, the immortal divine ruler."

The minions stood facing their leader with their arms held over their heads, waiting for him to tell them to put them down. They had not studied dictators and didn't know how long a salute lasted. They looked at their Eternal Guide with awe and admiration. In their minds, he was a genius. They were correct on that point. Dr. Morley was brilliant, but he was also stark-raving insane. Anyone watching the ridiculous activities in the time craft would realize that. His insanity would have been comical if he was not also dangerous and lethal.

"Where do you want us to go now Excellency?" the man at the craft's controls asked.

"This sequence and frame, Collin," Dr. Morley answered, giving the man a slip of paper.

The time craft landed in front of a single-story building on a deserted highway. It was the middle of the night, and the highway was dark. For security, the area around the building was well-lighted. Morley waved off his two minions when they started to get out the craft's cloak cover. "Forget it," he said. "We won't be here long enough to need it. Just put on your gloves and head covers." The two men followed Morley to the building's front door. "Break it in," he commanded them.

The two men raised their legs and with one combined kick the lock gave way and the broken door swung open. Immediately an alarm went off and the building's interior lights came on automatically. The two men in purple followed Dr. Morley into the building, ignoring the alarm noise. They were in a gun store. Glass cases full of rifles hung from the walls, while the pistols were displayed in a low case with a countertop. "Smash it," Morley said pointing at the case under the counter. The men reduced the front of the case to shards of glass lying on the floor.

"This is what we want," Morley said pointing at the weapons. The two men reached in and each took a large pistol. "No, not those," Morley corrected. "They are too powerful. Larger weapons are hard to aim and control. We need smaller ones. They work better up close. The dictators I studied assassinated lots of people, so I know what I'm doing. Take these." He reached in and handed smaller pistols to both his men. He took a third and stuck it in his pocket. "One more thing," he said. "Some of these." He snatched two small plastic boxes of ammunition and placed them in his other pocket. "Now, let's go."

The craft disappeared as two police cruisers with flashing lights and blaring sirens pulled up in front of the building. Two cops leaped out of each cruiser with guns drawn. Another car pulled in close behind. It was the store's owner. He had been notified by the alarm company about a break-in at his business. While the police examined the crime scene the gun shop owner rewound the store's security video. The four officers and the owner watched the monitor as the video played back. They were shocked to see a box-shaped object appear in front of the store. They were even more astounded when three small, human-like creatures with large black, oval eyes got out of the object. Two of the creatures were purple and one was red. They saw the creatures kick in the door and then smash a cabinet. They watched them take pistols and some bullets. Then, the creatures left, got into their craft, and it disappeared. "I think we should report this as a false alarm," one officer suggested. The owner and the other cops all nodded their silent agreement.

The stolen time craft set down in the desert. There was no one for miles. "I'm going to teach you to use these weapons," Morley told his minions. "Take these," he said, giving them ammunition. "Put them in here, like this." He loaded his pistol. "A projectile comes out this opening at high speed. Make sure you always point the weapon away from yourself. You make it work by pulling this small lever with your finger. Just point and pull."

Morley aimed his pistol at a cactus and pulled the trigger. There was a loud pop. A chuck of flesh flew off, leaving a gaping gash in the branch. "The weapon will do the same thing to a human," Morley explained. "To be sure you complete the job, you pull the lever again and again, as fast as you can. He fired repeated shots at the cactus. Pop, pop, pop. Each time, fragments flew from the poor mutilated plant. "When we approach Dr. MacDonald, do that. Over and over. We want to hit him as many times as we can. Try it."

The minions aimed and fired repeatedly. Most shots missed, but several found their mark. They stopped when the pistols clicked. "You need more of these," Morley told them, handing out bullets. The men reloaded and fired again. This time, even more chunks of cactus flew in the air. The pair stopped again when the pistols clicked.

"Hmmm," Morley said. "I only have three of these left. I didn't think this through. We need to go back for more. Into the craft." Teller stood at the pilot's console and looked inquiringly at Morley. "Back to that store," the would-be dictator ordered as he loaded the last three bullets into his gun. "Wait. Don't go back to the same frame. The police were arriving as we left. Find a sequence a short while later."

The time craft landed in the gun shop parking lot. Once again, it was late at night. The store was fitted with a new door. "Knock it down," Morley ordered. Once again the men kicked it in. Once again, the alarm sounded and the lights came on. This time, there was something new. A Doberman appeared and stood menacingly in front of the three burglars. It growled a challenge, revealing its long, white fangs. Teller and Bryant backed up and stood behind Morley. "You cowards," the man snarled in disgust.

He pointed his pistol at the dog and fired his last three shots. Pop. Pop. Pop. The dog yelped and fell. "Do that when you get in front of Dr. MacDonald. It will be a lot easier with him. The man is in a wheelchair. He can't move and he won't bite you. Now, take lots of boxes," Morley ordered his men as they smashed the display case.

Back in the craft the pilot asked Dr. Morley, "Where next Excellency?" Morley handed his man another slip of paper. "This sequence and frame." This time the craft landed on a grassy area beside a sidewalk. Looking out the portholes Teller and Bryant watched a group of young people walk by carrying books. Some of them wore blue sweat shirts with the white letters UNH on them. "This is the University of New Hampshire, where you work," Morley explained. "You don't recognize it because we're in Dr. MacDonald's time. He will be here soon. Wait until that group of students is gone and we will get out. Cloak the craft and move it behind that large tree."

Teller and Bryant easily lifted the cloaked craft and placed it where Morley had indicated. They walked away after finishing the job. "You fools," Dr. Morley hissed. "You didn't pay attention to where you put the craft. How will you be able to find it when we're done? Always make note of where you place the craft. It's a good thing I'm a trained S/O. Remember, it is behind *that* tree."

More and more groups of students walked by the invisible trio and into a nearby brick building. For decades Dr. Morley had observed Time Institute cadets do the same thing. "Students are coming from one class and going to another," he explained to his minions. "Wait a minute and we will see what we are here for."

Sure enough. Along came an older man in an electric wheelchair. He was surrounded by a group of students who were walking with him and chatting away. "It's MacDonald," Morley whispered to Teller and Bryant. "He's going to teach a class in that building."

"What should we do Excellency?" Bryant asked nervously, afraid to anger Morley. "These weapons are loud. Everyone will hear them."

"Don't worry, Lars," Morley whispered reassuringly. "We're not going to kill MacDonald here. It's too risky. I just wanted to see him." As the group passed out of earshot he spoke louder. "I have two plans. I really want to use the first plan, to kill him at the Hampton Summit. It would be so spectacular to assassinate him in front of all those world representatives. It would set off Chaos instantly and begin my empire with a bang." He chuckled at his own joke. "However, we will use the other plan because it is safe. Back to the craft and go here," he said handing Teller another slip of paper. "It is the Addison-Gilbert hospital in Gloucester, Massachusetts, 1901."

Normally a time craft takes off without causing any sensation. The crew doesn't know they are in flight unless the pilot tells them. They don't know they've arrived unless told. Everything is that smooth. Not this time. The stolen time craft lurched and pitched side-to-side so that Morley and his men were thrown around the cabin. "What was that?" Morley demanded of Teller. "*What was that?*" he repeated angrily when the answer did not come immediately.

"I… I don't know," Teller stammered. "It's not supposed to do that."

"Of course it's not supposed to do that," Morley screamed. "You fool. I was time traveling before you were born. I know it's not supposed to do that! Now, tell me why!"

Teller remained silent and slowly shook his head side-to-side. He did not dare make eye contact with the Eternal Guide. Bryant looked out a porthole and added, "We've arrived somewhere. Look," he said pointing outside the craft.

Morley peered through a window and spotted a large sign on the lawn in front of a brick building. "Well, you idiot," he hissed at Teller. "You managed to get us where we were going. It's the Addison-Gilbert hospital. Head covers and gloves. Cloak yourselves, cloak the craft, and place it behind that sign."

Inside the hospital the group looked around. Teller and Bryant were amazed. They had never seen anything so primitive as this building. "Follow me," Morley whispered, even though the lobby was empty. As the three tiptoed by the front desk, Morley noticed the calendar. It was September 22, 1901. Thinking perhaps the calendar had not been changed for a number of days, he checked a newspaper on the desk. The date was also September 22, 1901. "Back to the craft," he ordered angrily.

"I gave you a sequence and frame," the older man screamed at Teller, his pallid, wrinkled face turning red with anger. "You missed, you idiot. You got us here six days early!"

"I put in the frame and sequence you gave me," Teller pleaded. "I don't know what happened. Maybe that bump had something to do with it."

"Enter that sequence and frame again," Morley ordered angrily. "Take us to the right date this time."

Teller entered that sequence and frame and engaged the craft's drive. Nothing happened. "Maybe we've just jumped forward six days," Teller said hopefully. "We stayed in the same place, so it doesn't look like anything has changed."

"Lars," Morley said to the other man in purple. "Go into the hospital and check the date. Look for a newspaper."

"When Bryant returned, he shook his head side-to-side to indicate the bad news. "Same date," he said.

Morley exploded. "You idiot. You cretin idiot," he screeched at Teller. "You've damaged the craft." He pulled his pistol from his pocket and aimed it at Teller's head. His arm twitched repeatedly as he struggled between his desire to kill his minion and the realization he still needed the man. Teller covered his face, expecting at any moment to exit time and enter eternity.

After a while of indecision, Morley lowered his pistol. "I'm not going to shoot you now," he hissed. "But if you have messed up this mission, I swear I will. You had better believe me. I will kill you myself."

Morley sat on a bench to think. Bryant sat across from him, while Teller thought it best to stay at the pilot's station. It was as far away from Morley as he could get in the small craft. "Lars," he snapped at the minion sitting on the bench opposite him. "You're supposed to be the engineer. Fix this thing! Now!"

"Excellency, I only do maintenance. The engineers tell us what is wrong with a craft and we replace things that are broken. I'm not able to figure out what happened. I'm not really an engineer."

"You stupid, incompetent imbecile!" Morley screamed at the top of his lungs. He stood and banged his fists against the cabin wall. He kicked a bench. Then, he turned and tried to kick Bryant, who was fast enough to avoid the Eternal Guide's foot. Morley became so frustrated he sat back down and howled in anguish.

It took a long time, but eventually he calmed down and began to think out loud. "We have to wait six days and then do what we came here for. The problem is after. How do we get out of here? We need another craft... Oh no! Without MacDonald's discovery there will never be time travel and there will never be any more time craft. We've got the only one and it doesn't work. I need a time craft to make myself emperor. Arrrrrr...," he screamed while his minions cowered.

The next six days were not happy ones for the men waiting in the time craft. Morley made certain that Teller and Bryant remained miserable.

Chapter 17

Life at the Time Institute

The Time Institute was a lot like Atlantic

Academy. The cadets had homework and had to write

papers. They had tests. There was an important

difference. At the end of the day at Atlantic Academy

the students went home. At the Time Institute they

lived together in a dormitory. As a result, they were

constantly in each other's company. That was on

purpose. The Institute kept the cadets all in one

building so they would become friends. Someday, they would be on teams together. They would have to work well with each other and know they could trust each other.

Every night after supper the cadets gathered in the common room to study. Allie and her roommate Jen Canfield always joined the boys to form a study group. Jen was from New Zealand and spoke English with that country's accent. Her accent was so strong that when she got excited and spoke quickly, her friends could not understand her, even though she was speaking the same language. Jen had smoky gray eyes that she had inherited from her European father. Her skin was nut brown, a gift from her native New Zealander, Maori mother. Her eyes and skin created a striking contrast. Jen's hair was very dark, and she wore it short like a boy's. Like Patrick, Jen was good at math and was studying to be a pilot.

All the cadets took *Ethics* and *History* together. So, Patrick, Nick, and Jen spent part of every evening with Mike and Allie. Then, the groups of cadets rearranged. The pilots formed study groups with other pilots, while the engineers studied with their fellows. At 10:00 the cadets went back to their rooms. Classes started at 8:30 the next morning.

Rabbi Cohen's dominos had shown the cadets why their *Ethics* class was so important. Time traveler mistakes can have serious consequences. On the other hand, Dr. Newcomb also taught them that some time traveler mistakes were harmless, even funny. If a cloaked time traveler bumps into someone, he or she can be felt. If a time traveler speaks, his or her voice can be heard. If an invisible time traveler moves something, this can be seen. People thought ghosts were doing these things. Every country tells stories of small people with magical powers, like leprechauns in Ireland. These too were the result of time traveler encounters.

Mike raised his hand. "Dr. Newcomb, I know time travelers are visiting my time. Are people from the future visiting us now in this time?" he asked.

"Very good question, Mr. Castleton," Dr. Newcomb responded with his ever-present smile. "We have to guess that yes, they are here. After all, I am sure future people can still time travel, and I am sure they are still curious. Curiosity is such an important part of human nature.

"In the beginning of time travel we made some serious mistakes. That is why we have our ethical code. We are more careful now and we are always getting better at our jobs. I suspect the future has worked out all our problems. We don't know they're here because they don't make mistakes. I don't want to hurt your feelings, but I bet that in the future there aren't any Fixer teams, as there are no mistakes to fix. This is my own personal opinion. No one knows for sure, but I think that's the answer."

"I understand, Sir," Mike continued. "However, wouldn't it be a lot easier to go into the future and find out?" The class giggled at this question. Patrick and Nick slumped in their seats in embarrassment. Allie and Jen frowned as they looked around the classroom, angry at the other cadets for being so rude.

Dr. Newcomb held up his hand to tell the class to stop. "Please, do not let the other cadets hurt your feelings, Mr. Castleton," Dr. Newcomb explained. "You did not grow up in this time and are unaware of things they have known since childhood. Time travel has its limits. We can go back in time to any mapped sequence and any frame. We can return forward in time, but only to the frame we left. We call this the *frame of origination*. A time team leaving today can return to its frame of origination - today. A time team leaving a year from now can return to its frame of origination - a year from now. We don't know why we can't go beyond the frame of origination, but we can't.

"But Dr. Newcomb," Mike continued with a puzzled look. "Patrick, Nick, and I, we're not from this time. We traveled forward. How could we do this?"

"There is an exception," Dr. Newcomb replied. "You can be brought forward in a time craft. Since future time travelers have not come back to get any of us, we don't know anything about our future."

Each afternoon after lunch Patrick attended his *Leadership Development* and *Crisis Management* classes. The *Leadership* teacher was a retired pilot and had spent her career as a Researcher. She taught the cadet pilots about team identity. A good crew member cares more for the others than for him or herself. A good crew member will face danger for the team. A team will trust their leader as long as that leader is willing to do anything he or she asks a team member to do. So, Patrick and the other cadet pilots engaged in team building exercises. When they went rock climbing they tied each other's ropes. When they went skydiving they packed each other's parachutes.

Nick loved his two afternoon classes. Each day he couldn't wait for them to start and he was sorry when they ended. In *Time Craft Mechanics* he got to take a craft apart. He learned that the craft's hull is like very tough Styrofoam. That's why it weighs so little.

A craft has few moving parts and they work like muscles, not like gears and levers. The craft doesn't have a computer. Its human interface circuits act like small human brains. They learn, just as people do. This means a craft will develop a personality and will even form relationships.

"Hey Patrick," Nick said to his friend one night in the common room. "Did you know that a pilot and his craft form a bond?"

Patrick had not begun his field training, so this was news to him. "No," he said in surprise. "Tell me more." Mike, Allie, and Jen all looked up from their books to listen.

"My teacher said a time craft is like a race horse and the pilot is like its jockey," Nick explained. "A horse and the jockey learn from each other. The horse knows the jockey's signals and runs best for its own jockey. Another jockey can ride the horse but won't get the same results.

"My teacher says an engineer and a craft are like that same horse and its trainer. They form a connection too. The trainer takes care of the horse. He feeds it and cares for it. The horse and its trainer love each other. It's the same for an engineer and a craft. So, a craft works best for the engineer it knows."

Nick's normally worried face had a look of pride, knowing he would be an engineer someday. "The Time Institute gives a pilot and an engineer one craft, for as long as they fly. The pilot and the engineer bond with their craft. When they retire, the craft is recycled. They don't give it to a new crew. My teacher says S/Os come and go. The pilot, the engineer, and the craft are always together."

Nick looked at the disappointment on Mike's face. He felt left out. His two friends would always be together, while he was like a spare tire. "Not Fixer S/Os," Nick reassured him. "Fixer teams are always together. They all have the same job. Mappers and Researcher S/Os have specialties. So, they change when the mission changes. Allie's specialty is music. So, she wouldn't go on mission to study a battle." Nick looked at Allie. She had the same expression as Mike. "Sorry, Allie," said Nick. He decided to clam up.

Nick's fourth class was *Innovative Emergency Repairs*. Like Patrick's *Crisis* class, Nick studied case histories. He learned about engineers that had saved their missions by solving problems. The engineer cadets were taught the same repair and then practiced it over and over, learning to do it quickly. In an emergency they could make the fix under pressure, even under difficult conditions.

Mike and Allie took *Methods of Observation,* a boring class where S/Os were taught to notice details. Mike described his *Methods* class to Patrick and Nick. "You remember the puzzles we did in grade school? You had two copies of the same picture and you had to find ten things that were different. A lady's shoes were red in one picture and blue in another? That's the sort of stuff we do," Mike complained. "It's not very exciting."

Practical Scientific Application was even worse. S/Os learned to keep records, and this meant filling out forms. "It's called *Practical Scientific Application,*" Mike told his friends. "I don't know what application it has to science. And it certainly isn't very practical."

Five weeks into the term, Patrick came into in the common room and found Mike and Allie. They could tell he was excited. "You won't believe what I did today," Patrick said. "I made my maiden voyage." Mike and Allie didn't know what that meant. "I flew in a craft, not as a passenger, but as a pilot-trainee. I stood beside the pilot as she showed me what to do. I programmed the craft. There was no one else with us, just the engineer.

"From now on, I'll be the one to fly the craft to the sequences and frames. The pilot's gonna let me take over more and more. Right now, I'm a pilot third class. I'll become second class when I fly a mission by myself. When I solo with just an engineer, I become pilot first class."

Nick showed up just as Patrick finished. He was excited too. "Guess what I did today? I flew as an engineer-trainee. We went back to a sequence and frame where we had a simulated emergency. I worked with the engineer while he made the repair. He even let me calibrate. It was great. It was just the engineer, me, and the pilot."

"Let me guess," Mike said. "You're an engineer third class right now. From now on you'll be doing more and more of the repairs. When you're ready, you'll do all the repairs yourself. The engineer will only watch. Then, you'll be engineer second class. Someday, you'll travel alone with just a pilot and an S/O and you'll fix the craft all by yourself. You'll become engineer first class."

"Yeah," answered Nick, crestfallen and deflated. "How do you know?"

Allie pointed her thumb at Patrick. "He told us."

"Don't take it personal, Nick," Mike said to his friend. "We're jealous. You guys get to go on real missions while Allie and I do simulations. They train S/Os in this hologram theater. We watched Columbus get off the Santa Maria and into a row boat. We recorded the details. Then, we watched him land on the beach and claim the island for Spain. We recorded those details too.

"You know, the guy was kind of ugly," Mike said.

"He was boring too," Allie added. "If I was going to claim an island, I would have been more dramatic. She stood. "I claim this island for Queen Isabella and King Ferdinand of Spain!" she said throwing back her long auburn hair. She held out her left arm and pretended to drive a flag pole into the sand with her right.

Patrick and Nick laughed at her acting. "Guess what we are," said Mike with a grimace. "We're S/Os third class. When we're ready, we observe a simulated mission all by ourselves. Then, we become S/Os second class. We don't get to go on a real mission until the test for S/O first class."

Chapter 18

Risk

Three months into their term Nick came into the common room after his last class of the day. Mike and Allie were waiting for supper. "I did it," he announced to his friends. "I'm Nick Pope, engineer second class. I made my mission today. The craft's gravity polarizer broke so the craft couldn't fly. I had to fix it, but I couldn't lose the craft's charge. We would have been without power."

Mike and Allie were impressed at Nick's new rank. He continued his story. "We were in London in the Middle Ages, during a plague. A couple of times I had to go outside to work under cloak. The gloves and head gear made it harder."

"What would have happened if you couldn't make the repair?" Allie asked.

"The engineer-trainer was right there," Nick answered. "This time she didn't say anything. I had to do it all by myself. I had to figure out the problem, and I had to figure out how to fix it. She was there if I got into trouble. I don't know what would have happened if I lost the charge. We can only get power at the black hole. Anyway, I didn't. So, now I'm second class."

"Why London during a plague?" asked Mike.

"The trainer said she wanted the test and the conditions to be difficult. I watched the Londoners. They were in a panic. I saw some awful things. Lots of them were dead. If the people had seen me, I would have scared them even more. They would have thought I was a demon or the angel of death. So, I had to make the repair without violating Time Institute ethics. But I pulled it off."

Nick had just finished when Patrick and Jen arrived from their last class of the day. "Nick is engineer second class," Allie announced to them.

"Congratulations, Nick," Jen said. "How does it feel?"

"It feels good," replied Nick. "You guys must be close to your test."

"Two days from now. Day after tomorrow," answered Jen. "I'm getting nervous. Were you?"

"Oh, yeah," confessed Nick. "I'm really glad it's over and I can relax. I was so nervous I didn't even tell you guys – just in case I flunked."

"Yeah," responded Patrick. "I wasn't going to bring it up, except you asked."

"We're being tested this week too," Allie added.

"But we're still going to be in the hologram theater," said Mike. "If we mess up we'll only be embarrassed. I'm jealous. You guys do actual missions. It's not fair being an S/O."

"That's what you guys get for being so brainy," said Nick. "Do you know what it's like hanging around with a couple of S/Os? Half the time, we don't know what you're talking about."

Mike crumpled up a sheet of paper and tossed it at Nick's head, causing the group to break into laughter. When they calmed down Nick became serious. "I'm sorry, Allie and Jen, but I have to talk to Mike and Patrick about your time."

"Go ahead," said Allie. "I won't be upset. Remember, I'm an S/O. My job is to observe and learn. If you've discovered something important I want to know it."

"I need to know it too," Jen added. "Go ahead. Don't let us bother you."

Nick spoke in a low voice. "The other cadet engineers and the trainers I work with, there's something missing. They're not open to anything new. They don't experiment. They don't try things. They don't wonder what would happen if you did something different."

Nick leaned in toward the others. The group all put their elbows on the table and moved in toward him. Anyone walking by would know this was a private conversation. "I'm taking a course called *Innovative Emergency Repairs,* but I'm not learning anything innovative. They know how to fix things, but that's all. They have a method for everything, but it's all stuff they learned from missions that went bad. It's memorization of what to do if something goes wrong. That's why we read case studies. If A happens, do B because that's what so-and-so did once, long ago.

"I don't know what they would do if something new went wrong. I don't know if they could figure it out. It's almost like they don't know how to think though a problem, only how to copy.

"I worked all summer with my grandfather restoring that sports car and we had to figure out all kinds of things. My grandpa is really clever and innovative. He just comes up with things out of his head. If it doesn't work, he tries something else. If he can come up with a better way, he does that. He can look at something he has never seen before and figure out how it works, and how to fix it.

"Take the cloak," Nick said. "They can cloak the craft from inside. Outside they have to use that cover. Mr. Smith hoped the engineers will come up with a way to turn on the cloak from outside. No one has. Why? How hard can it be?"

"I've been thinking something similar," Patrick added, speaking in the same loud whisper as Nick. "But I thought I was the only one, so I didn't say anything. Piloting is all rules too. Everything they do, they've been doing for a long time. There's nothing new. I made some suggestions, but the trainer told me to stick to their ways. Don't take risks she said.

"If I talk to the other cadet pilots about risk, it's like they're afraid of it, or they don't know what it is. They're happy to do things the way they've always been done. Don't do anything new. Don't take any chances. That's the rule."

"I guess necessity really is the mother of invention," Mike said out loud as his mind and mouth made another of their connections.

"Huh?" asked Nick. The others looked at the S/O with curiosity.

Mike realized what had happened and lowered his voice to the same loud whisper. "You know the old saying 'necessity is the mother invention?' Human beings have always been innovative. They figured out how to do things because they had to. It was a matter of surviving, or not surviving. This society is so rich and safe no one needs anything. There's no necessity, so there's no reason for innovation. There's no reason to take any risks."

The group was silent while they pondered Mike's answer. "That's very interesting," said Jen. "I've never noticed that we're not innovative. I've never even heard anyone talk about it. Just you guys. Was it really that different in the past?"

"We talk about human nature in *Ethics* class, in *History*, and in *Methods*," Allie added. "We talk about human curiosity and about human will, but no one ever talks about innovation or risk. I wonder if we've lost that ability."

"A fish doesn't know it's wet," Mike added, as another one of his thoughts slipped out. The others said nothing. They just looked at him, knowing he would explain it.

Mike looked around at his friends. "I did it again, didn't I?" he asked. Everyone nodded. "It's something my father says. A fish doesn't know it's wet. Allie and Jen, you don't see the things we see. We're from outside this time, but you grew up in it. You accept that things are the way they are. You grew up swimming in this lake." The girls nodded their heads.

"You guys have given us something to think about," said Jen. "Someday, you'll leave and go back to your sequences, but Allie and I will still be here. I guess it'll be up to us to get people thinking about innovation and risk."

Two days later Patrick and Jen came into the common room where Patrick dropped himself into a chair. He threw his legs out in front of him, spread wide. Jen didn't sit, but paced nervously back and forth. "Pilots second class," she told the others with a look of relief. She began to speak rapidly as her excitement over took her. "What a mission! I flew the craft all by myself to the black hole."

Allie held up her hand, a gesture that told her roommate to slow down. The others could not understand her strong New Zealand accent. "Oh," Jen said. She took a deep breath to calm herself and began to speak slowly and deliberately. "I docked and recharged. Then, I flew to a specified sequence and frame."

"I did the same in my craft," Patrick added. "I went to Genghis Kahn's camp. I was right in the middle of his army as he was getting ready to attack. I landed without being seen. We waited and watched the soldiers out the portholes. Then, I returned – all by myself."

"Next step – solo," Jen announced.

"That's great," Allie said with disappointment. "Today, Mike and I watched Polynesian woman weaving baskets and drying fish."

"We did such a good job observing they made us S/Os second class," Mike added with disgust.

Chapter 19
The Briefing

One afternoon Jen came into the common room and looked around for the boys. She found them sitting with Allie. "Patrick, I have a letter for you," she said giving him the message. She sat next to Allie. Everyone was curious and watched Patrick as he examined the envelope.

"Open it," said Nick. "See what it is."

Patrick looked concerned as he silently scanned the communication. Then, he read it aloud, *"Mr. Weaver: Please report to Room 307 at the MacDonald Center tomorrow afternoon at 4:00. Please bring Mr. Pope and Mr. Castleton with you."* The note was signed by Dr. Newcomb.

"What do you think they want?" Nick asked, looking even more worried than normal. Anyone could tell this note had upset him.

"Have we done something wrong?" Mike asked. He was as worried as Patrick and Nick. Each looked around at the others and shrugged. No one had any ideas. They just shook their heads.

Patrick, Nick, and Mike arrived at Room 307 early. If they were in trouble, they didn't want to add tardiness to their crime. The door was closed, so they waited quietly in the hall, listening to their hearts pound loudly in their ears.   At 4:00 the door opened and Dr. Newcomb stuck out his head. "Won't you cadets come in?" he asked. As the boys entered Room 307 they realized it was a conference room, like the one in front of Miss Watson's office. Mr. Smith was sitting at the table. They were surprised to see Mrs. Alvarez, the Atlantic Academy lunch lady sitting next to him. She wore a gray Fixer uniform and nodded to them.

There were three empty chairs across the table from the adults. Dr. Newcomb gestured to the seats and asked them to sit. "Let me tell you why we are all here," he said with his ever-present smile. "It occurred to me after I sent my note that it might sound ominous and cause you to worry. Please don't. Everything is fine."

"We weren't worried," said Patrick shaking his head. Mike and Nick did the same, but they were just being polite. They had been nervous all night and all day. This was a relief.

"Let me begin by reassuring you that we are pleased with your progress," Dr. Newcomb continued. "You are doing better than we hoped. You three cadets are all receiving excellent grades. Your field trials are even better. Mr. Pope, your emergency repair during the London plague received the highest score by an engineer second class in 37 years. I can tell you that Miss Watson was the last engineer to score that high."

"I hope that doesn't give away her age," Mrs. Alvarez added, smiling and winking at Mr. Smith. "She's a bit sensitive about that." Mr. Smith smiled and nodded knowingly.

Nick was embarrassed by the recognition and the compliments. He looked down at the table and murmured, "Thank you."

"You have been here four months," continued Dr. Newcomb, still smiling. "In three months, you will complete your term at the Time Institute. You will be fully trained and ready for your mission. Today, we will brief you on that mission. We are going to tell you all we know and give you your plan."

Mr. Smith held up a picture for the boys to see. "This is the target - Dr. James MacDonald," he said. "You should know what he looks like, in case you get near him. As you can see, he is confined to a wheelchair. That makes it easier to identify him.

"This is Dr. Roger Morley," he said, holding up another picture. "I told you about him in Miss Watson's office, but that was several months ago. So, I will review for you. Dr. Morley was a teacher here at the Time Institute. All of us know him. He was one of our best. He was a great scholar and the cadets loved him. He was also a good Researcher S/O.

"Several years ago, Dr. Morley developed a brain tumor. Surgeons removed it. It seems to have come back and has taken over his mind. He has gone insane. He developed a condition called megalomania and decided he would become a dictator. However, he doesn't want to be an ordinary dictator, and control only a country. He wants to control the world.

"His plan is pure evil. Dr. Morley intends to assassinate Dr. James MacDonald. That way, the Hampton Summit will never happen. The world will go on like it had for thousands of years, continuous war and most people hungry. The world will run out of energy, and technology will disappear. Dr. Morley plans to use war, hunger, and poverty to take power.

"By killing Dr. MacDonald, Dr. Morley will change all the main time sequences. We can't imagine the Chaos he will cause. He doesn't know the consequences either, but he is willing to accept the risk."

Mike thought to himself, "At least someone in the future is willing to take a risk." He put his hand over his mouth. He didn't want to think that thought aloud.

Mr. Smith continued. "One of our time craft is missing, as are two maintenance workers. We know Dr. Morley promised them important jobs in his new dictatorship.

Here are two more photographs," he said, passing the pictures to Patrick. "These are the two missing men. The one on the right is Lars Bryant. The other is Collin Teller. "Mr. Castleton, they are what you call *the minions.* Mr. Bryant and Mr. Teller are strong men," Mr. Smith warned. The boys looked at the photos. The two maintenance workers did look strong. They wouldn't want to mess with either one of these guys, never mind both.

"Mr. Teller and Mr. Bryant work on time craft. Their job is to fix things and make test flights. So, they have some done some piloting and engineering. But you are better trained, and are more skilled. We think Mr. Teller is acting as pilot with Mr. Bryant as engineer. Dr. Morley is the S/O. That is the time team you will be hunting. You and your crew should study those pictures," Mr. Smith advised Patrick. "You want to recognize all three on sight."

Mrs. Alvarez addressed the boys next. "You were surprised to see me," she said. "I'm Mr. Smith's S/O. I've been working at Atlantic Academy with him and Miss Watson. I've drawn up a plan. Here is a list of the most important frames in Dr. MacDonald's sequence." She passed the list across the table to Patrick. "If he is killed before any one of these frames he will not make his discovery. The Hampton Summit will never happen. You need to visit each of these frames. Do it in the order I have listed. It's a safe, risk-free way to find where Dr. Morley is going to attack."

"Risk-free," the boys thought to themselves without expression. "Safe and risk-free, but not very innovative."

"So, we locate Dr. Morley and his minions," asked Mike. "Then what?"

"We rely on you," Mr. Smith replied, as if the answer was obvious. "That's why you were chosen. Miss Watson, Mrs. Alvarez, and I watched you closely. We know what you are made of. Your rock version of *All Hail Atlantic* proved it. You have what Miss Watson calls audacity. You're innovative and take risks. I'm afraid that is something we don't do well. We're careful and cautious, but that won't work in this case."

The boys were stunned, and tried not to show their amazement. If the Time Institute knew it had a problem, why didn't they change? Mike figured they just didn't know how.

"Fixer teams would face two difficulties," Mr. Smith continued. "I told you about one of them in Miss Watson's office. We can't always stay cloaked on a mission like this. Uncloaked, we would stand out. Any little thing could trip us up. It could be as simple as an expression, or a slang word. We would make a mistake and everyone would know we didn't belong there. So, we need someone who can blend in. You grew up in that time. You know everything you need to know."

"We're fish that swim in that lake," Mike said, another of his thoughts slipping out. He put his hand over his mouth.

"In a way of speaking," Mr. Smith answered with a puzzled expression. He ran his finger tip over his mustache thoughtfully. He didn't understand what the reference to fish meant. "Second problem," he continued. "Dr. Morley is one of us. He trained with us and he has served on missions with us. He knows how Fixer teams work. He knows how to hide from us and how to outsmart us. But he doesn't think the way you do. You have audacity, and you can surprise him."

Patrick looked at his crew, and then he looked across the table at Mr. Smith. "Okay," he agreed. "Let's say we find Morley and his guys. Now, we have to stop them, and we have to bring them back. What are we going to use for weapons?"

The three adults were shocked and looked at each other in surprise. Dr. Newcomb's smile disappeared as he leaned forward on the table. The boys knew he was serious and meant for them to listen carefully. "We don't have weapons," he said almost in a whisper. "There have been no weapons for longer than anyone can remember. We don't have to defend ourselves, and we would never attack anyone. Any weapons we have are in museums, and they don't work anymore."

"What do you expect us to do?" Patrick asked with surprise. "These guys aren't going to give up because we scold them and tell them they're being naughty."

Dr. Newcomb remained serious. "Dr. Morley's plan is pure evil. However gentlemen, fighting evil is never an excuse to use evil. Wrong can never stop wrong. Only good can beat evil. Only right can beat wrong. You must be good, and you must be right. Dr. Morley and his minions are willing to kill millions of people and enslave the rest. But you cannot cause their deaths. If you were to use weapons you would risk hurting or killing innocent bystanders," the Ethics teacher continued. "If you do that, you change their sequences. You will have violated our ethics and caused Chaos. Gentlemen, remember what I taught you. Never do any harm. There is no wiggle room here. You have to bring Dr. Morley, Mr. Bryant, and Mr. Teller back alive. You cannot cause them any serious injury."

"There is good news," Mr. Smith added. He forced a smile, as if he were trying to make the boys feel better. "Dr. Morley and his minions don't have any weapons either. Even if they did, they wouldn't know how to use them. You're on a level playing field. You will take on Dr. Morley with your wits, not with weapons," he said trying to sound encouraging.

The room went silent. The boys couldn't think of anything more to ask. The adults had said all they had to say. Patrick knew the meeting was over and stood up. "Please excuse us, we have homework to do," he said as he put the photos in the envelope. The adults nodded and remained seated as Mike and Nick followed Patrick out of the room.

The boys walked out the MacDonald Center's front door and touched the bronze plaque an extra-long time. "We'll need all the luck we can get," Mike muttered.

On the way to the bus stop Patrick asked his team, "Do you feel like we were just given a bunch of contradictory orders? Follow this safe plan, but be audacious. Stop these really strong guys from destroying the world, but don't hurt them."

"I think they're being unfair," replied Nick. "Did you see Bryant and Teller? They could twist us into knots. We can't use weapons because we might hurt them? I'm worried about them hurting us."

"My mother says 'It's easier to get forgiveness than permission,'" said Mike thinking out loud. The other two waited for him to explain. "They gave us a plan. Let's say we don't follow it, but we still manage to stop Morley. Do you think anyone is going to make us sit in a corner? We're not supposed to hurt them, but let's say we rough them up a bit. Do you think we'll get sent to our room without supper? No. Success is all that matters. I vote we bring those guys back anyway we can, and the heck with the plan."

"Whoa. You are audacious, Mr. Castleton," said Patrick, teasing his S/O.

Chapter 20

The Mission Begins

The last two months of the term were hard work. Teachers piled on the assignments and field training intensified. While studying, cadets would place their heads on the table and fall asleep. Friends would elbow them to keep them awake. This is the reason the Institute kept the cadets all in one dorm.

The class had bonded together and no one would let a classmate fall behind.

Seven months after the boys arrived from Atlantic Academy the class graduated. All the cadets' families and friends came. Patrick, Mike, and Nick were the only ones alone. Mike thought about his parents and his home. He had been so busy he had forgotten about them. He realized his parents had no idea where, or when he was. For them it was still 3:45 on a January afternoon. They thought Mike was at Atlantic Academy in detention with Miss Watson. Boy, he said to himself, time travel does mess with the mind.

After the graduation ceremony Mr. Smith found Patrick and his crew. He didn't waste time on congratulations or small talk. He said straight out, they were now a Fixer team and it was time for their mission. They should leave the next day. He used the same joke he had used at Atlantic Academy. "As you know, there is no time like the present."

The boy's didn't laugh. Mr. Smith's words were too sobering. Instead, each spent a moment alone with his thoughts. Patrick, Nick, and Mike always knew that someday they would leave on their mission, but that day had always been in the future. Now it had arrived, and it took the fun out the graduation celebration.

That night there was a party at the dorm. The boys smiled and had a good time with their friends, but they knew that in the morning they would be gone. Mike took Allie outside the dorm where it was quieter and told her the news. Tears welled up in Allie's eyes, but she quickly dried them. She was a member of a time crew and couldn't cry. "I will miss you Mike," she said, regaining control of her emotions. "I wish you, Patrick, and Nick all the best. I hope your mission, whatever it is, is a success."

She took Mike by the hand and led him back into the common room, where the rest of the evening, she appeared to have a good time. Sometimes, Mike saw her smile disappear and she became momentarily serious. Then, she would catch herself and force another smile. Mike knew the smile was a mask hiding Allie's true feelings. It was tough leaving her, but he felt better knowing she would miss him.

At 8:30 the next morning the boys walked to the arrival/departure pad. In the distance they could see a row of new time craft, lined up and waiting for their recently graduated pilots and engineers. At one end of the row they spotted a small group of people waiting for them. Mr. Smith had come. So had Miss Watson, Dr. Newcomb, Rabbi Cohen, and Mrs. Alvarez. Mike's heart skipped when he saw Allie and Jen standing with the adults.

Patrick and Nick walked up to the group. Meanwhile, Allie stepped aside and Mike went to her. "What are you doing here?" he asked gently. That didn't sound right. He added, "I mean I'm really happy you're here, but how… why?"

"Dr. Newcomb invited me and Jen," replied Allie. "He knows we're all friends. He didn't tell us what you're going to do. He just said we should be here. He's so nice."

"Yeah," Mike answered. "I'm really glad you're here too. When we said goodbye last night I didn't think I would ever be with you again."

"I know. I'm worried about that too," replied Allie. "We're from different times and we have our own sequences. I guess we should have never met, but we have. It hurts to think of not seeing you anymore."

Allie held a small, square box in her hand. She opened it and lifted out a locket. "Here," she said to Mike as she put the chain around his neck. "I'll never forget you Mike Castleton. I hope this will help you to never forget me." She showed him the locket's cover. *Remember Me* was engraved on it. Allie opened the locket to show Mike the picture inside. It was them. He remembered the night Jen had taken it. Mike had put his arm around Allie's shoulder and pulled her close so their heads touched. Jen must have given the picture to Allie.

Mike smiled a bittersweet smile, both happy and sad at the same time. He tucked the locket inside his uniform shirt. He took both of Allie's hands and held them as they looked into each other's eyes. "Goodbye Allie," Mike said. "Let's promise never to forget each other. Let's do everything we can to get back together somehow, some time."

"I promise," Allie said as she leaned forward and kissed Mike on the cheek.

At that moment the two realized everyone else was watching them. The adults smiled at the two young people. All of them had said goodbye to special friends as they left on missions. They understood what Mike and Allie were going through.

"Way to go, Big Guy," Patrick teased.

"Come on, Romeo," added Nick. "We've got a mission waiting for us."

Mike let go of one of Allie's hands. Holding her other, he walked her back to the group. "I'm ready," he said. He looked at Allie again and slowly let go of her other hand. Jen put her arm around Allie as the three boys turned and walked to their craft. It was the first one in the row.

Patrick stopped in front of the craft to examine it. He had the same expression Mike did when he looked at Allie. "She's a beauty," said Patrick with a broad smile. "Look, on the front. CT 9225." He turned to Mr. Smith. "What's that stand for?" he asked the older pilot.

"That's the production number. It doesn't mean anything," Mr. Smith replied, running his finger over his thin mustache. He smiled at Patrick's appreciation of his new craft. Mr. Smith was a pilot too and understood Patrick's pride. "A pilot gets to name his craft. You can give it a name if you want."

"I like that number," Patrick answered. "It feels lucky to me. I'll keep that as its name."

"You have a factory charge, enough power to get to the black hole," Mr. Smith advised. "There, you need to give the craft a full charge."

While Patrick and Mr. Smith talked, Nick walked around the CT 9225 like a proud father. His smile was so wide it erased his normal worried expression. He fell instantly in love with the new craft. He promised it and himself, it would be his baby. He would pamper it. He would get to know the craft inside and out and give it the best of care.

Mike waited patiently while Patrick and Nick got excited about their new craft. He was an S/O and didn't feel any of these emotions. For him, a time craft was like a bus. You get on, and when you get where you're going, you get off. Patrick approached the craft door and answered the math question. "Seventeen," he said. The craft door opened and he stepped in. Nick and Mike followed.

The pilot and engineer were as awed by the craft's interior as they had been of the outside. They gazed around and examined every detail, looks of admiration and love on their faces. Finally, Nick sat on the bench behind Patrick. The pilot stood in front of the tiny screen, next to the open door. Mike sat on the far bench so he could look out the door and still see Allie. He felt a lump in his throat as he blew a kiss to her. She smiled sadly and waved. Jen hugged Allie.

Patrick looked at the screen and answered the math joke. "2B, or not 2B," he said. "Hah. Is that ever lame! Give me something funnier next time," he told his craft. The joke may have been old and worn out, but it worked. The keypad appeared and Patrick programmed a trip to the black hole. He was about to engage the hyper-light drive when he realized he had not closed the craft's door. He blushed at his mistake.

"Ooops," he said to his friends. "That was bush league."

Patrick answered the addition problem that would close the door. As he spoke Allie broke away from the adults. She bolted forward and dove head first through the opening. She tucked her shoulder and did a somersault across the craft's floor coming to a stop when she slammed into the far wall, her head on the floor and her legs in the air.

Before the boys could react the door closed and the craft had begun its flight. The adults outside were so surprised they never moved. They watched Allie spring forward and into the craft and saw the door close behind her. Immediately, the craft disappeared from the departure pad.

"Allie," Nick yelled. "You put us overweight."

Mike helped Allie off her back. "We're in flight," Mike replied to Nick. "We can't be overweight. You know, you're so skinny and Allie is so small, I bet we're still under the limit, even though we've got four people in here."

"I've got to take her back," Patrick said with a frown and shaking his head. He was not happy that his mission had started off with a problem. He had enough things to worry about without an added complication.

"Why?" Mike demanded.

"Because this is a dangerous mission," Patrick answered. "I don't want to be responsible for someone else. We've got enough on our plate."

"Allie's had the same training we have," Mike argued. "She graduated with honors, just like we did. I say we could use another person. She makes it four of us against three of them, and I like those odds a lot better. I wish we could have brought our whole class with us."

"The three of us were picked because we're audacious and take risks," Patrick persisted.

"Did you see what Allie just did?" Mike fired back. "You don't think that was audacious? You don't think she took a risk? She's got guts, just like we do."

Patrick tried one last argument. "She wasn't briefed," he said without a lot of conviction in his voice.

"Jeez," Mike said tossing his hands in the air as he dismissed Patrick's final feeble attempt. "Don't you think *we* can take care of that?"

Patrick looked at Nick for support. Nick shrugged his shoulders. He didn't have any arguments left either.

"Okay," Patrick said with resignation. "Welcome aboard Allie. Welcome to the mission.

Mike, it was your idea. Brief her. Meanwhile, we're off to the wormhole."

Even before Mike had told Allie the whole story she understood why the mission was so critical. "This is incredible," she said, her eyes wide open in disbelief. "If Dr. Morley assassinates Dr. MacDonald he'll set off a wave of Chaos that will roll through time. My world will be destroyed."

"It will be just like the falling dominos Rabbi Cohen showed us," Nick answered. "If Morley murders Dr. MacDonald in our lifetimes, the Chaos will wipe out our futures too. He destroys everything for our families, and for our friends."

"He shreds the future for our kids," Mike added, as he pondered growing up in the world Morley was planning.

"We've got to stop him," Allie said fiercely, with a steely look in her eyes. "I will sacrifice my own life if I have to."

"I'd call that guts," Mike said glancing at Patrick.

Patrick sat on the bench next to Nick. Mike and Allie sat together on the other bench holding hands. The cabin was silent. The mission was finally under way. It was really happening. Each sat quietly, thinking his or her own thoughts. At last, Mike spoke. "About Mrs. Alvarez's plan, I have some ideas." Allie turned to face him while Patrick and Nick looked up to listen. "If I were Morley, I wouldn't risk taking on Dr. MacDonald himself," Mike continued. "We know these Time Institute guys. They play it safe, and there's a lot safer way to get him out of the way." Patrick nodded to show he was listening. Both he and Nick leaned forward, toward Mike.

"I'm sure if I know about the Grandfather Paradox, Morley knows it too," Mike said. "It would be a lot safer for him to knock off Dr. MacDonald's grandfather than to assassinate the man. That way, Dr. MacDonald never exists. He doesn't make his discovery and there's no Hampton Summit. Famine and war go on and Dr. Morley rules the world. I think it's something he would try. It's an old idea and it fits the Time Institute mentality. Don't be innovative. Above all, don't take risks."

"OK. If we go this route, how do we find Dr. MacDonald's grandfather?" asked Patrick.

"I already did it," Mike replied with a self-satisfied smile. "While we were at the Time Institute, I went to the library and looked up Dr. MacDonald's family tree. James Allen MacDonald was born in Gloucester, Massachusetts, January 7, 1953. His father was Neil MacDonald. John MacDonald, Neil's father and James' grandfather, was born in Gloucester, September 28, 1901. John lived 68 years and died in Gloucester, March 5, 1969.

"Dr. MacDonald had two grandfathers," Patrick replied. "How do we know Morley won't go after his mother's father?"

"That's too innovative," replied Mike. "Time Institute people are predictable. I'll put my money on John MacDonald. He has the same last name as Dr. James."

"It makes sense to me," added Nick. "What else do you know?"

"John – whose nickname was Jack – was born in the Addison-Gilbert Hospital. In 1924 he married a woman from Nova Scotia and the couple ran a candy business."

"How sweet it is," joked Patrick.

"I suggest we go to Gloucester the day Jack was born," Mike continued. "I doubt Morley would go back any earlier in the family. It's called the Grandfather Paradox, not the Great-Grandfather Paradox. We'll make sure Jack was born, and then we go to the frame when he should die. If he died earlier than he was supposed to, we know where and when

Morley attacked. We go back to that frame on Jack's sequence and we stop Morley there.

"If Dr. MacDonald's grandfather dies at the proper time, we'll know Morley didn't go after him. We'll have to go back to Mrs. Alvarez's plan," Mike concluded.

"You've really thought this thing through," said Nick. "When did you come up with all this?"

"After our briefing," answered Mike. "I didn't tell you guys. I didn't want to take any chances of our teachers finding out."

"Thanks," said Patrick with an annoyed frown. "You don't seem to trust us a lot."

"No," Mike responded, reassuringly. "It's not that. We were almost never alone. I didn't want to take the chance of someone hearing us. I figured we would never be more alone than we are now, and this would be the safest time to talk."

"Yeah, I suppose it was good thinking," said Patrick. He shrugged his shoulders and dropped his frown. Nick nodded his head.

The boys fell quiet again. Nick looked even more worried than normal, like he was working up his courage to speak. "I have a thought," he announced at last. "At the Institute, I learned that time craft can be seen by radar. I asked my trainer why they don't use stealth technology, like we do on military planes. They're not interested. They don't care if radar sees them; they just don't want people to see them."

"I don't get it," said Patrick with a puzzled look. "Are we gonna find Morley with radar?"

"No. That was just an example," Nick answered. "I'm thinking night vision goggles, the infrared kind, the ones that see body heat. If we had night vision goggles I think there's a pretty good chance we could see Morley and his men, but they wouldn't be able to see us. It would give us a major advantage."

"It would be a lot easier if we could see them," agreed Patrick, nodding his head.

"Where would we get night vision goggles?" asked Allie.

"I've seen them in a store that sells telescopes and binoculars," Nick replied. "We don't have any money, so we can't buy them. We could steal them, but that's a problem with ethics. I wouldn't want anyone stealing from me." Nick paused a second, knowing his friends were going to be stunned by his second option. "The other place is the military," he added.

"The military?" asked Patrick with a laugh. "They're not going to give us goggles. Wouldn't we have to steal from them too?"

"I think of it more as borrowing," said Nick. "We would return them when we're done."

"Okay. Where and how?" Patrick asked.

"There's a National Guard armory in Portsmouth," Nick replied. "It's near an auto parts store I went to with my grandpa. Sometimes I saw soldiers around, but I didn't see any security. I figure we can get inside if we're invisible."

Patrick gave Mike and Allie a look that asked for their thoughts. "We can't use weapons," Mike shrugged. "We're gonna need every advantage we can get. If this works, it would be huge. I think we should go for it. What have we got to lose? Time?"

"We could get caught. We could change history," Patrick answered.

"We're chasing Morley because the Time Institute isn't innovative," argued Mike. "They told us to be audacious, to surprise Morley. That's what we do best. As for history, it's our time. We won't be changing anything."

"OK," Patrick replied. "I'm sold. I'll change Mrs. Alvarez's plan for our time, Portsmouth, New Hampshire. It'll be easy to look up that sequence. Mr.

Smith has it the directory. After the armory, we'll head for Jack MacDonald's sequence. I'll bet some Mapper team has recorded it in the directory too. After all, he's Dr. MacDonald's grandfather. In history he's a pretty important guy.

"I figure we start with Jack's first frame, when he's born. We'll head there when we get back from the wormhole. Rip up Mrs. Alvarez's plan, Mike. We won't be using it." Patrick made two changes to the program. The first was for Portsmouth today. After they got the goggles, they would be off for Gloucester, September 28, 1901.

Patrick sat back down next to Nick, facing Mike and Allie on the other bench. He looked serious. "In my Leadership classes the teacher told us that a good crew makes a good leader. I want you guys to know that in my book you're the best. Thanks for your support. Thanks for the time you put into thinking this stuff through; you make it a lot easier. We really are a team."

Patrick returned to the pilot's station. "Come see this," he said to the others. They looked out the front window and in the distance they could see the wormhole. The CT 9225 flew into its open end. The inside of the wormhole whipped by in a blur, like the craft was flying through a tunnel. Mike, Nick, and Allie weren't scared. Patrick was one of the top pilots in their class.

Patrick guided the craft out the wormhole's far end. The others looked out a window and could see the power plant near the black hole. Patrick docked the craft and got out. His crew watched him talk with the maintenance workers. He showed them his pilot's I.D. card. The workers hooked cables to the craft and began charging it.

When the maintenance crew was done Patrick shook hands with them. He waved good bye, and returned to the CT 9225. He flew the craft a safe distance from the power plant, and then went to hyper-light speed and reentered the wormhole. Allie and the three boys were headed for 21st century Earth.

Mike and Nick lay back on the benches and relaxed while Allie leaned her head on Mike's shoulder. Mike wished the craft had a CD player so they could listen to music. He would like to play Allie some of his favorite songs. He heard Nick start snoring as the engineer took a nap. He heard Allie breathing deeply and steadily too. Their breathing made Mike sleepy, and soon he drifted off as well.

Mike woke suddenly. He had felt something like a gentle bump. His movement startled Allie, who sat up too. They looked out the window and saw that Patrick had landed. However, they didn't see Portsmouth. They seemed to be in a desert. Mike reached across the craft and poked Nick to wake him. "Where are we, Patrick?" he asked a little worried.

"No sweat," Patrick answered. "We were in the neighborhood, so I figured we should stop by and visit a place we've always wanted to go. Ladies and gentlemen, welcome to Mars. We're the first people here."

Chapter 21
Mars

"Wow," Nick said with so much excitement that for a moment his usual worried expression disappeared. "We're on Mars. I can't believe it. NASA's still on the drawing boards, and we're already here."

"We always wanted to be the first people on Mars. Now we are," Patrick added with a proud grin.

Mike and Allie looked out the port holes on their side of the craft. "It really is red," Allie said.

"It's a nice place to visit, but I wouldn't want to live here," Mike joked.

"Then how about a short vacation?" Patrick responded. "Anybody want to explore?"

"We can't do that," Mike warned, suddenly becoming very serious. "I studied Mars. Its atmosphere is so thin we can't breathe it. It's also freezing cold out there. I don't know if we would suffocate first, or freeze to death. Either way, it'll happen pretty fast."

"I already figured that out," Patrick replied with calm reassurance. "We have these uniforms. Remember what Mr. Smith said? They will protect a time crew in space long enough to get rescued. If we put on the head gear and gloves, we should be able to spend a little time on Mars."

The others looked at each other and shrugged. They couldn't think of any reasons why not. In their full uniforms Mike and Nick looked at each other and burst into laughter. "These big, dark lenses make us look like bugs," said Nick. "No wonder people think time travelers are aliens."

They all touched the panels on their chests and felt the suits pressurize. Patrick stepped to the control panel to open the door. "Patrick, I don't know what's going to happen," Mike warned. "Remember, there's a lot less atmospheric pressure out there than in here. We could get sucked out the door when you open it."

"What should I do?" Patrick asked.

"Read the math question, but don't answer it right away," Mike advised. "First, come back here with the rest of us and grab on to the benches. Then say the answer. When the door opens, we won't be near it."

"Will do," agreed Patrick. He read the problem and stepped back to hold on. "Thirty-two," he called out. The door opened and the time travelers felt themselves pulled towards it as the air rushed out. Then suddenly, the air stopped moving. The group stood up. "Lead the way, Mr. Scientist," Patrick told Mike, who stepped out onto the Martian surface.

"That's one small step for a kid," Mike said theatrically. "That's one giant leap for all kid kind."

"You idiot," Patrick said to his S/O as the other three stepped out behind Mike. They paused a moment while the enormity of their accomplishment sank in. Their feet were actually on Martian soil. This wasn't a game played in the woods. This was the real deal. They had done it. They were only twelve years old and their life-long dream had been realized. They were the first people on Mars.

The group moved carefully away from the craft. With each step, they bounced up like they could float. "Whoa. I feel so light," said Patrick.

"You are," Mike responded. "You weigh about 38 pounds. Mars is much smaller than the earth, so it has less gravity. At Space Camp I learned how to travel in low gravity so you don't get tired. Watch me. This one's called the Bunny Hop." Mike put his feet together, and bent his knees to jump. He took off and traveled a distance longer than his body. He landed and hopped another time. In only a dozen hops he was a long way from the group.

"It's easy," he called back to them. Nick, Patrick, and Allie heard him clearly, even though the Martian atmosphere was too thin to carry sound very well. They realized their head covers had microphones and earphones. "Of course," Patrick said to his friends. "A crew has to be able to communicate if it's lost in deep space. There's no air in space to carry sound. So this is how they do it."

Mike called back to the others. "This move works too." He pushed off with one foot and took a long floating step. It was like Mike was running with springs on his feet. A dozen of these springing steps brought Mike back to the group. "If you move like that you won't get tired as quick," he repeated. "You'll get where you're going a lot faster too." Nick, Patrick, and Allie tried the same steps. It took a little practice but soon, they were all traveling easily across the Martian surface.

Patrick took the lead. "Are we heading west?" he asked Mike, pointing to the sun.

"Yeah, it's mid-afternoon," responded Mike. "Mars turns the same direction as the earth, so that's west. The sun will set over there."

"Good," said Patrick. "We need to remember where we went. We have to find our way back."

"We're leaving footprints," said Allie. "We can follow those too."

The group hopped for a while as they climbed a small ridge. At the top of the rise they looked back to realize Patrick had landed the CT 9225 in a basin. They were higher than the craft, so they would have no problem finding it again. Patrick led the others out onto another flat area about as wide as a football field, with another ridge in the distance. "Let's see what's over that rise," Patrick said. Off they hopped, faster than they could run on earth.

They climbed the next rise and found themselves on another flat area. It was like the group was climbing wide Martian steps. Patrick continued to bunny hop straight ahead until suddenly he stopped and waited for the others to catch up with him. The pilot pointed at the dirt. "We're not the first ones here," he said in surprise. In front of him was a pair of wheel tracks, like those made by an all-terrain vehicle. "Is it real aliens?" he asked.

Mike studied the tracks and walked beside them for several steps. "You know, I'll bet those were made by one of the Mars rovers. We must be near a landing site. Let's see if we can find it. I studied these things. I've read everything I could find about them. They traveled very, very slowly – about ½ inch per second. At that speed it can't be too far away."

"These tracks go in both directions," Nick observed. "We don't know which way it went. We could go the wrong way and never find it."

"It went this way," said Allie pointing to their right.

"How can you tell that?" asked Patrick, surprised that she was so certain.

"She's an S/O," Mike replied. "She's a trained observer. So am I. See that rock with the small circle cut into it? The rover has a rock abrasion tool for taking samples. Since the tool is on the front of the rover, it was facing that way when it took the sample.

There's no sign it turned around, so it went in that direction," he said, pointing again to their right.

"I'm impressed," said Patrick to the two S/Os. "Let's track it down." The pilot hopped in the direction Mike had pointed. The group had not gone far before Patrick stopped again. He had spotted the rover. They stood still and watched it for a while, but it didn't move.

"You know these things were only supposed to work for 90 days," Mike whispered.

"I don't think it can hear us," said Patrick in a normal voice.

"Yeah, right," Mike replied, a little embarrassed. "But we want to make sure it doesn't see us. It has cameras front and back. For safety, I suggest we circle around and come at it from the side."

Patrick led the group off to the right in a long loop. "The rovers went on running for years," Mike continued. "They're a real credit to NASA. Those guys kept figuring out ways to keep them going. I heard on the news a while ago that NASA had finally lost one of them."

The group approached the rover's right side. Allie was surprised by how primitive the machine looked. It had lots of moving parts. None of them worked with human interface circuits or simulated muscles, like a time craft. The boys were surprised at how big the rover was, about the size of an ATV. It was flat like a V-shaped skate board. It had two masts, a tall one in the middle and a shorter one on the front.

Close up, the group could see that the rover was covered by a thin layer of fine dust. "Rovers ran on batteries," said Mike. "Every day when the sun comes up all those flat solar panels charged the batteries. NASA figured that someday Martian dust would cover the panels. Not enough light could get through and the batteries would die."

Nick examined the rover more closely. "That's not the problem," he said. He pointed out a tiny dark smudge at the edge of a small door. "That spot was caused by a short circuit. Good thing the air is so thin. On earth that fire could have burned up the rover. There's so little oxygen here it went out right away. I bet that short is what killed the rover, and I think I can fix it," he said. He pulled a small box off his waist and held it up for the others to see. "It's an emergency repair kit. All engineers carry them. There's a bigger kit in the craft, but this one has to be on my belt all the time."

Nick opened the small door and looked inside. "There it is," he said. He stepped back so the others could see. They didn't know what to look for, so Nick pointed out the problem. "There's a piece of sand caught right there. It caused a short circuit. It isn't much, but it did in the rover." Nick reached in with a tool like a pair of tweezers and removed the sand. He took another tool out of his kit and reached through the door to do something else. "That's it," he announced with satisfaction. "This thing's ready to get back on the road." He returned his tools to his kit and closed the door. "You know more about this rover than I do, Mike. If I understand, this thing's batteries will recharge from the sunlight. Right?"

"Yup," Mike answered. "The batteries will charge faster if we wipe the dust off the solar panels. I bet by tomorrow morning NASA gets a signal from it. Won't that be wild? They thought it was dead, and suddenly it comes back to life."

"They can't discover that someone did it for them," Allie warned. "NASA would think aliens fixed their rover. We need to remember our ethics."

"Right," replied Mike. "The rover has cameras, but they won't work until the batteries charge. We'll be long gone by then. I'm sure the NASA engineers will use the cameras to examine the ground around the rover. We can't let them find our footprints." He bent over and began to smooth out the dirt with his hands. "Help me," he told the others. "We'll get rid of all the prints around the rover. Then, we'll back out the way we came. We'll wipe away those tracks too."

The four backed up brushing the ground in front of them and leaving a trail of fresh dirt. Mike said the trail was too faint for the cameras to see. "Even if they do see it, they won't think it was done by humans," he explained. "They'll think it was wind, or something. The planet has an atmosphere. It's thin, but there's wind. In time, the wind will blow away all the evidence of us being here..." Mike's voice tailed off like something troubled him.

Patrick and Nick bunny hopped back to the craft. When they got there, they discovered Mike and Allie were not with them. Concerned something had happened, they hopped back to where they had last been together. At the top of the rise they looked out on the flat where Mike and Allie had scratched out in the dirt:

"PW NP AT MC
WERE HERE."

Mike and Allie were carrying basketball-sized stones and were placing them end-to-end on their message. Patrick and Nick realized right away what they were doing and picked up rocks to help finish the project. "The wind will blow away our footprints so no one will ever know we were here. This will last forever," said Mike with satisfaction. "This will be our monument. It will always prove we were the first people on Mars. We worked hard to make it happen and I want the credit. People may not know who we were, but they'll sure know we were here first."

The youths finished the monument and climbed the next rise to look down on their work. "That's big," said Mike. "So big, someday a satellite could take a picture of it. It's written in English, so they'll know we weren't aliens. It's sure gonna make NASA scratch its head," he said.

"I don't know how long these uniforms are good for," Allie added. "We better not take any chances."

The group hopped back to the craft and Patrick opened the door. Nick went in and sat down where he had been before their arrival, on the bench facing the opening. Allie stepped in and sat across from him. Patrick waited behind Mike. However, Mike didn't climb aboard. He stood in the doorway, staring at Nick.

"What are you doing?" Nick asked him.

"Beam me up, Scotty," Mike said to the engineer.

"Huh?" asked Nick, confused.

"Beam me up, Scotty," Mike repeated.

"You can just step in," said Nick, wondering why the S/O was acting weird.

"Never mind," Mike replied, annoyed that the engineer didn't get the joke. He climbed into the CT 9225 and sat next to Allie.

Patrick stepped in, took his place at the control panel, and closed the door by answering an addition problem. Safe inside the craft he reached for his head cover. "Stop!" Mike yelled. Patrick turned and looked at him. So did Nick and Allie. "Patrick, you haven't pressurized the cabin. It's the Mars atmosphere in here. You'll die if you take that off."

"Thanks," said a frightened Patrick, realizing a bullet had gone by his head.

"Pressurize the craft," Mike said to the pilot.

There was a long uncomfortable pause. "They never told me how," admitted Patrick. "I don't even know if it's possible. Maybe these craft don't pressurize." He looked at the others. Even though they couldn't see his face, they knew Patrick was scared. They could hear it in his voice. They felt the same fear wash over them. The four were stranded, and they had stranded themselves with their own foolishness. If only they had stuck to the mission they wouldn't be in this mess.

They were silent for a long time as they wrestled with their problem. At last Mike spoke. "I have an idea, Patrick. Take us to earth. We'll pressurize there."

"There's a partial vacuum in here," said Nick. "I'm not a scientist. But if we fly into earth's atmosphere, won't there be a lot more pressure outside? We could crush like a tin can."

"Outer space is a vacuum," Allie noted. "We don't explode from the pressure inside."

"Yeah, but you can't count on that," Nick replied. "The craft may hold pressure in, but not out. Boats are built to keep water out, but not in."

"Humm," thought Mike. "You're right. We don't know. After all, it never dawned on us these things couldn't be pressurized. We'd better not take the chance."

The craft was silent again. "I have it," Mike announced. "We'll pressurize slowly, in stages. Patrick, get us to earth as fast as you can and stop in the outer atmosphere. Shoot for about 10 miles up. I'm glad I paid attention at Space Camp."

"When we get there I'll have to guess at how high we are," said Patrick. "This thing doesn't have an altimeter. We're using this craft in ways it wasn't designed for."

At time craft speed, the flight didn't take long. At earth, Patrick slowed down high in the atmosphere. "Can you come to a full stop, Patrick?" Mike asked.

"Yeah," Patrick replied, not sure what Mike was planning.

"This is my idea," Mike explained. "We're up really high, but there is still a bit more pressure outside than here inside. We'll open the door and equalize. Then, we close the door. We drop down a bit more and come to another full stop. We'll open the door there, and we'll get even more pressure in here. If we do that all the way down, we should pressurize gradually. Once we get near the ground, we'll be okay." Patrick opened the doors and closed them again. Then, he flew the craft lower in the atmosphere. Again, he opened and closed the door. He did this several times.

Finally, he looked out to see the ocean not far below him. Mike looked too, and said, "We're almost at sea level. We can take off these head covers." Mike removed his and took a deep breath. "Yup. It's clean, fresh ocean air. You can smell the salt." The other three pulled off their head covers and breathed a sigh of relief. They had escaped a close call.

"Where to now?" Patrick asked Nick.

"Portsmouth, NH," answered the engineer. "The National Guard armory is on Market Street. Do you have the coordinates?"

"Yup," responded Patrick. "All programmed in." He patted the place in front of him where the keypad was located. The gesture showed Nick he had already done the job. Seconds later Patrick announced, "We're here." He set the craft down in front of the armory. There was a driveway on the right, so he chose a spot out of the way, on the lawn. He didn't want anyone to bump into the cloaked craft.

"This was your idea, Nick. What do we do now?" Patrick asked his engineer.

"We should wait for night," Nick replied. "I think all the guardsmen go home after work. When it's dark, we can get out of the craft without being seen. We'll wait outside and sneak into the armory tomorrow morning when they open the doors."

"I'll see you tonight," Mike said, taking Allie's hand. He lay back on one of the benches and nodded off. Allie put her head on his shoulder and closed her eyes. Patrick and Nick curled up on

opposite ends of their bench. In minutes the entire
crew was asleep.

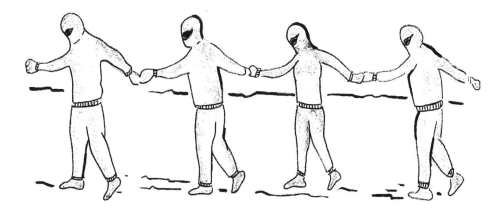

Chapter 22
Night Vision

Patrick woke first. He didn't know the time, but it was now dark. He elbowed Nick and called to Mike and Allie. "Let's go," he said. The group put on their headgear and gloves. They touched their chests to turn on their cloaks and each saw the others disappear.

"You there?" asked Patrick.

"Yup," three voices replied.

"Cloak off," Patrick said. The four all appeared again. "This isn't gonna work," he explained. "How are we gonna communicate? I can't speak to you, or they'll know we're in the building. I can't see you, so we can't use hand signals. What do we do?"

"I don't know," said Nick.

"Do like Mike and me," Allie said lifting up her hand. She lifted up Mike's along with it. "Hold hands to make sure we stay together."

"Holding hands is a good idea," said Patrick. "But if we go in four across we're gonna take up a lot of space."

"No, not side-to-side," Allie replied. "Front-to-back."

"Like elephants in the circus, trunk holding tail," Mike explained. "We each stick one hand forward and the other back." Mike held out his arms to show what he meant. "We'll be in line, so we can go down corridors and through doors."

"Good idea. Nick should take the lead," said Patrick. "I've never been in a storage area."

"My grandpa and I have been in lots of them, buying parts" said Nick. "Things are stored a special way that makes them easy to find. Let's get outside the craft while it's dark. We'll wait out there for the soldiers to show up in the morning."

Patrick opened the door. "Get the cloak cover," he said to Nick and Mike.

"No need," Nick replied as he tossed Patrick something small and black.

"What's this?" asked Patrick. "It looks like a cell phone."

"It is," answered Nick. "Anyway, it used to be. I used Mike's phone to make you a cloaking remote."

"Thanks," said Mike, very annoyed. "I had been looking for that."

Nick didn't pay any attention to the unhappy S/O. "I put a mental interface circuit in it," he explained to Patrick. "The circuit is the same as the ones in the craft, but smaller. To use it, you hit *Send*, just like a phone. That calls the craft. The craft sends the math question to the phone and it shows up on the screen. You answer it by speaking into the phone. It's real simple.

"You can do the same thing to open the door. It will come in real handy if there's an emergency. You know, if we have to get into the craft real fast. You can open the door from a distance. You don't have to be standing next to it anymore."

"Awesome," was all Patrick could say as he admired Nick's invention. "This is awesome."

Mike continued to grumble about his phone as the group stepped out of the CT 9225. They were in a city and there was enough background light to see their craft, even though it was night. "Twenty-one," said Patrick into the phone. The ship cloaked. "Wow," the pilot said in amazement. "I'm really impressed. This gives us another advantage over Morley."

"Yeah, really impressive," Mike mumbled with a frown, still upset about losing his phone.

"We need to cloak ourselves again," Patrick said. "We don't want to be seen hanging around an armory at night. That will attract attention." The four disappeared. They took each other's hands and walked around the CT 9225 with Nick in the lead. He kept his free hand on the invisible craft to keep from wandering away from it. "I don't know how long 'til sun up," said Nick. "But we might as well get some more sleep."

"One of us has to stay awake," Patrick warned. "For security, in case anyone comes by. Let's take shifts. I'll go first. You three take a nap. Mike, I'll wake you in a while. Then, you can keep watch."

"OK," replied Mike. "Nick, remember it's a secret we're here. So, don't snore."

"I don't snore," Nick said.

"You do too," Mike insisted.

"You snore a lot louder, Mike," said Patrick. "I spent seven months in the dorm listening to you. You were going at it so heavy one night I put a pillow over your face. You never even moved. You didn't stop either."

Patrick remained awake on lookout while Mike and Nick snored next to him. "At least Allie is quiet," Patrick thought to himself. Before his time on guard duty was up he noticed a soft rose color in the eastern sky. It told him the sun was coming. There was no sense in waking Mike for such a short watch. He let his friends sleep while he enjoyed the sunrise.

The light of dawn was so pale everything was in shades of gray, but Patrick could see that trees in the distance had leaves on them. They had left Atlantic Academy in the winter when the trees were bare. He must have been slightly off in choosing this frame, and had arrived either earlier or later in the school year. He would have to wait for more light to determine what month this was. He would know once he could see the color of the leaves. In spring, fresh, young leaves are light green. Dark green leaves would mean it was summer. A bit of red or yellow would indicate late September. That's when leaves change colors in New England. In October, they begin to fall off the trees. There was enough light to tell that hadn't happened yet.

He wondered how he could have made this mistake. It didn't matter this time, but on future missions missing by seconds, never mind months, could be dangerous. Patrick realized where he had goofed. When they changed Mrs. Alvarez's plan he had replaced the setting with one of Mr. Smith's. For some reason, Mr. Smith must have come to this month. Patrick would have to be more careful, but for now there was no harm.

As the dawn grew brighter Patrick could see red and yellow leaves, meaning it was late September. At home, he was just getting out of bed to get to his morning math class. He wondered what the day's assignment was.

The rising sun awoke the other three. "Good morning," Patrick said. "Sleep well?"

"The ground is hard," groaned Mike. "I'm stiff."

"I'm hungry," said Nick. "And thirsty too."

"That's what that is!" Mike exclaimed. "That feeling in my stomach, it's a cross between pain and gnawing. I'm hungry. You know why I didn't recognize it?" he asked his friends, as the answer dawned on him. "After seven months at the Time Institute, we just spent a night in our own sequences. We're no longer having the experience of time. They're right, time travel does mess you up."

"We'll have to tough it out," Patrick advised as his stomach growled too. "We can't go looking for food now. We'll get the night vision goggles, and then we can take care of breakfast. I'm not sure how, but we'll it figure out."

The group waited as the sun continued to rise and illuminate their surroundings. Allie looked around in wonder at this strange time with its strange buildings, made of strange materials. Everywhere she looked there were lines of wooden poles with parallel wires running along their tops. She was surprised that people would live with something so unattractive. She noticed lots of ugly colored signs. Even through her head cover she could smell dirt and chemicals in the air. This was not the clean air she had grown up breathing. The only time she had smelled air this stinky was in the chemistry lab at her school in Ukraine.

As the sun rose above the distant trees a car pulled up in front of the armory and stopped. A soldier in army fatigues got out and opened the gate. She had three stripes on her shoulder, showing she was a sergeant. She drove through the gate, parked her car, and walked up the front steps. She tapped a security code into the alarm key pad, and unlocked the door. She hooked the door open and went inside.

Nick decided this was their chance and stood up. As he did, another car pulled into the drive. Nick and his friends froze while a man got out of the car carrying a newspaper. He walked up the steps and dropped the paper in front of the open door, and left.

The coast clear again, Nick moved forward. Like a parade of invisible elephants the group walked across the lawn and up the steps. On the landing, Mike hissed a low "Psst." The others looked down. The newspaper headline read *NASA Hears from Long Dead Rover.* They all laughed quietly.

The group walked carefully along the Armory's main corridor. It had rows of doors on both sides. Most of the doors had glass windows that let them see what was inside. They passed an office on the left where the sergeant sat at a desk, writing. A room on the right side had arm chairs and a coffee pot. It was the staff lounge, where the soldiers relaxed on break. The next door on the right was the motor pool. Humvees and military trucks were lined up in there.

At the end of the corridor were two metal doors without windows. One door had a sign that read *Authorized Personnel Only*. Nick pointed to the sign. "I'll bet that room is for weapons and ammunition," he whispered to his friends. "We want the other door." He tried to turn the knob. It was locked.

"Oh great," Patrick said softly. "Just our luck!"

"Not a problem," said Nick, letting go of Patrick's hand. "Stay put so I can find you again," he told his friends. "I can open the door, but I'm worried about an alarm."

"If one goes off, we're all on our own," Patrick instructed. "Scatter and meet back at the craft." The others couldn't see Nick. Had they been able, they would have watched him take a small tool out of his kit. They would have seen him put the tool in the keyhole and slowly twist it. They did hear a soft click as Nick picked the lock. They heard the knob turn and saw the door begin to open.

Nick held his breath as he gently pushed the door. No alarm. Maybe there wasn't one, or maybe the sergeant had already turned it off. No matter, the time travelers were in the supply room. Nick reached beside the door and found the light switch. He turned it on and the others entered. Then, he quietly closed the door behind them.

"They taught you to pick locks at the Time Institute?" Patrick asked in surprise.

"No," answered Nick. "My grandpa did. We got locked out of the house one day and he picked the lock to get us back in. I thought it was cool, so he showed me how.

"Mike, Allie" said Nick changing the subject. "Stay at the door and listen for footsteps. Patrick and I will look for night vision goggles." Nick led Patrick into the supply room. The place was huge. It had rows and rows of shelves, full of boxes from floor to ceiling. Patrick looked at all the rows, all the shelves, and all the boxes and thought of a needle in a hay stack. "Usually, they list stuff in a catalog," Nick told him. "When they want to find something, they look it up. The catalog tells them where it is. See if we can find the catalog. It's usually someplace central."

The two boys walked up and down several rows before Nick quietly announced, "Here it is." At the end of a row was a shelf, slanted forward like a desk. It had a large book on it, a pad of paper, and a pen. The pen was attached by a chain. "The pen and pad are so you can write down the catalog number," Nick explained to Patrick. "That way you don't forget the number while you're looking for what you need."

"Like in the library," Patrick said.

"Yup," answered Nick. "Just like the library." Nick opened the catalog and began searching for night vision goggles. At that moment Allie heard footsteps and voices in the corridor outside the door. She squeezed Mike's hand as a signal. Mike knew the room had been dark when they came in. That meant the lights were always turned off. Anyone entering and finding the lights on would be suspicious. He and Allie were standing right in front of the switch. He turned and flipped it. Then he guided Allie to the other side of the door. When it opened, they would be behind it. That way, the people outside wouldn't bump them when they reached for the switch.

Lights going out was a warning to Patrick and Nick that there was a problem. They dropped to the floor and rolled under a row of shelves. Each lay on his back. The door opened and the lights came on again. In walked two guardsmen wearing army fatigues. One was a corporal with two stripes on his shoulder. The other was a private with just one stripe. "We should start over here with the letter A," the corporal said to the private. "You count. I'll check off."

"Oh, no," Nick thought to himself. "They're gonna take inventory. They'll be in here all day counting the stuff in the boxes."

Nick was right. The private opened a box in the first row, the row marked with a large letter A and began counting its contents. The corporal had a clipboard with a computer printout. When the private was done counting, the corporal checked his list to make sure it jived with the items in the box. The two soldiers slowly worked down one side of the first row. Then, they worked their way up the other side. Then, they moved onto the second row marked with the letter B.

Patrick and Nick stared at the soldiers' boots close to their heads. All they could do was lay still. They were safe, as long as they stayed quiet. After an hour they were getting pretty stiff. Nick had been thirsty when they arrived. Now, his throat was bone dry. He swallowed to keep it wet, but even that was getting harder to do. Soon, all he could think about was a cold glass of water.

Poor Mike and Allie had the worst of it. They were still standing beside the door. Their legs and feet hurt, but all they could do was quietly shift their weight from one side to the other.

Two hours later the corporal and private finished the items that began with F. "I could use a cup of coffee," said the private.

"Me too," answered the corporal. "Let's finish one more letter. Then, we'll knock off for a coffee break."

The private began counting the items that began with the letter G. "Gas Masks," he announced. Long pause while he counted. "Thirty-nine," he said.

"Check," the corporal replied.

"Gloves, Winter," the private said. Another long pause while counting. "Thirty-eight.

"Check," the corporal repeated.

"Goggles, Dust." Again, a long pause. "Thirty-seven," the private announced.

"Check," the corporal added mechanically.

"Goggles, Night Vision." Nick put his hand over his mouth as he gasped. What luck! The soldiers had just told him where to find the night vision goggles. "Thirty-eight," the private said after a long pause for counting. The soldiers finished the letter G and left the room.

"I'm here," Nick whispered as he rolled out from under the shelf. The others felt their way until they found Nick with their hands. He was standing in front of the box of night vision goggles. "Each take a pair," Nick said. "Put them under your uniform shirt so they can't be seen. Someone will notice if four sets of goggles float down the corridor and out the door."

The other three did as told. Then, they took each other's hand and turned for the door. They couldn't feel Nick's hand. They looked for him even though they knew they couldn't see him. All they did see was a pen rise in the air and stand on its point. Then, it wrote on a clipboard. "Nick," called Patrick in a whisper, "What are you doing?"

"I'll explain outside," Nick answered. "Let's get out of here while we can."

Nick opened the door a crack and looked out. The coast was clear. The four slipped into the corridor, formed their elephant parade, and started for the front door. As they did, the corporal and private came out of the lounge and started to walk down the hall towards the invisible time team. The four pressed themselves against the wall just as the sergeant came out of her office. "How's it going?" she asked the other two soldiers.

"We'll be there the rest of the day, Sarge," replied the corporal. It looked like the three soldiers were settling in to chat for a while.

"You two see that game last night?" asked the sergeant.

"Yeah, it was great," answered the private. "I think the Patriots could go all the way this year."

"They will if they keep playing like they did yesterday," replied the sergeant.

"That interception in the third quarter with a 75 yard return. That was unbelievable," added the corporeal.

"That poor tight end from New York. He didn't know where the ball went," said the private.

"What about the Celtics?" the sergeant asked. "You think they can pull it together?"

"It's gonna be rough," replied the corporal. "They just don't have the height. They don't have the talent."

The three talked for another five minutes about the Red Sox and their chances of locking in the American League East wild card. Finally, the corporal said it was time for him and the private to get back to work. At that point the group of time travelers got another lucky break. If the soldiers walked down the corridor side-by-side, one might bump into them. Instead, the private stayed to talk with the sergeant while the corporal walked back to the storeroom, right down the middle of the corridor. When the private finished talking, he did the same. They both passed right by the four invisible bodies pressed against the corridor wall.

The two soldiers went into the storage room and closed the door, but the sergeant didn't return to her office. Instead, she turned and walked out onto the porch in front of the armory, blocking the door. She stretched and took a moment to enjoy the warm September sunshine. The group stayed put and waited for her to move. She did not take long. She watched some cars go by, and then she went back to her office and closed the door. The invisible youths looked into the office as they walked by. The sergeant was back doing paperwork.

Nick led the other three out the armory's front door, down the stairs, and across the lawn to the craft. "I can't open the door," said Patrick. "The craft will uncloak. Someone might see it."

"Do it," said Nick. "We'll jump in as soon as the door's open. The craft will cloak again when you close. It will only be visible for a couple of seconds. If anyone sees it, we'll be gone before they can check it out." Patrick took out his cell phone and sent a message to the craft. The math question appeared on the screen. He read it and spoke the answer into the phone. The door opened, and one after another, the four time travelers leaped in. Patrick was last. He closed the door and cloaked the craft as fast as possible. "Let's get outta here," said Nick.

In seconds the time craft was far away from the Portsmouth National Guard Armory. The four uncloaked so they could see each other, and then pulled off their head covers and gloves. "You promised me we'd get something to eat," Nick said to Patrick. "I gotta have something to drink. My throat's like a desert."

"Where can we go for food?" asked Patrick helplessly. "I don't have any money."

Mike and Allie shrugged to show that they didn't have any ideas. "Wait," Mike said suddenly. "This is today."

"Yeah. Like duhhh…," Patrick replied mockingly. He thought Mike's comment was stupid.

"No. I mean this is our time," Mike answered, ignoring Patrick. "You guys and me, we're at school right now. That means we can go home for lunch."

"We can't go to my house," said Patrick. "My father works at home. He'll ask why I'm not in school. He'll want to know why I'm dressed like this."

"My house is in a real close neighborhood. We'd be seen," added Nick.

"Well, my parents are at work and my house is in the woods," Mike said with satisfaction. "Take us there, Patrick. The only one home is my dog Menlo, and he won't tell."

Patrick landed the time craft on the lawn behind Mike's house. Mike found the spare key hanging on a nail under the porch rail and opened the kitchen door. Menlo rushed up to greet his master. He wagged his tail so forcefully it thump, thump, thumped against the door.

"Hi Mennie," said Mike, stooping and hugging his dog. "It's been a long time since I saw you." He looked at the clock and realized he was in his first class at Atlantic Academy. "But it's only been an hour since you saw me," he said with a laugh. "You don't understand, but time travel messes with your mind."

Next, Menlo greeted Nick and Patrick. He stopped when he noticed Allie, a stranger. "Mennie, this is my friend Allie," Mike told his dog. Menlo's tail started to thump against the refrigerator as he looked expectantly at Allie. She stooped down and greeted the dog, who began to bathe her face with kisses.

"You are loveable," she said as she took the dog's head in her two hands and rubbed his cheeks. That was it. Allie was now a beloved friend. Menlo stayed close by her for the rest of the visit.

Mike went to the refrigerator and took ice cube trays out of the freezer. He loaded four tumblers with ice and filled them with tap water. "This water's from a well. It's gonna taste great. No chemicals," he said holding up his glass to toast his friends. The other three clinked their glasses against his. They tipped the glasses to their mouths and drained them. Patrick and Nick held out their empty glasses to Mike so he could fill them again.

"Peanut butter and jelly?" Mike asked his friends. Allie had a blank expression. She didn't know what this food was. Nick and Patrick both nodded. The sandwiches disappeared fast. Allie smiled her approval of this newly discovered delicacy. Mike took down a basket from the top of the refrigerator. "Here are some chocolate chip cookies," he said to his friends. He explained to Allie, "PB&Js and chocolate chip cookies are my daily diet." His three friends dug into the cookies too.

Mike cleaned up and put the dirty dishes and glasses into the dishwasher. "Will your mother notice the extra dishes?" asked Patrick.

"Naw. I always make myself a sandwich when I get in from school," Mike answered. "She'll think I put them there." He paused a moment and added with a smile, "But I guess I did."

The four rested a while in the kitchen chairs. They had been through an exciting morning. At last, Patrick stood up and said with a serious expression, "We've got a job to do. We've gotta find Morley." Mike and Allie took turns bending over to give Menlo a kiss and a hug. Mike locked the kitchen door and pulled it closed behind them. Menlo jumped up to look through the window and watched the group walk across the lawn.

Inside the craft Nick said, "We should see if these night vision goggles do the job. Cloak yourselves." The other three put on their head covers and gloves. They touched their chests and disappeared. Nick put his goggles on his head and turned on the switch. He could see his friends standing in front of him in a pale gray light.

"Bingo," said Nick happily. "Morley can run from us, but he can't hide. I can see you guys as clear as day." The others put on their goggles but said they couldn't see anything. "You need to turn them on," Nick explained, as he showed them the switch. Suddenly, for all four, the world was an eerie black and white and gray. The night vision goggles didn't show color, but they showed everything else in detail.

"Morley doesn't have a chance," Patrick grinned. "All we have to do is find him."

"Hey Nick," said Mike. "I meant to ask you. What did you write back at the armory?"

"I signed out four sets of night vision goggles," Nick answered. "You always do that. If you take something from inventory you always sign it out.

That's how you keep track of what you have and where it is."

"You told them that Nick Pope took four sets of goggles?" asked Mike.

"Yes," replied Nick. "We have to return them when we're done. We still follow Time Institute ethics, right?"

"Right," agreed Mike and Patrick together.

"Our next step is to start looking for Morley," Patrick said. "We start in Gloucester, Massachusetts in 1901. I already have the Addison-Gilbert hospital programmed in."

Chapter 23
The Baby Killers

Patrick set the CT 9225 down on the lawn in front of the Addison-Gilbert Hospital. He had arrived in the middle of the night so the craft and crew wouldn't be seen. To be safe, he chose a spot behind the hospital sign. The group put on their night vision goggles and stretched their head covers over them. They stepped out of the craft and onto the lawn where the goggles turned the night into colorless daylight. They could see everything, even at a long distance.

"Look," Patrick said with surprise. "Morley's craft. They're already here." There on the lawn right next to theirs, was a cloaked time craft. Through their goggles the four could see the cloth cloak stretched over it.

"Remember, we can see them, but they can't see us," Nick told his friends.

"They must be inside," said Mike with urgency. "We had better get in there. We don't want to be too late."

The four youths jogged across the lawn to the front steps. The steps were made of wood, so they climbed carefully to avoid squeaking. There was no one around, but they thought they should be cautious anyway. They tried the front door. It was unlocked. They pushed it open and entered. Patrick looked down the corridor and noticed all the floors were wood. "We could make a squeak with every step," he thought to himself.

The others stared over Patrick's shoulder. This hospital was very different than any other they had been in. The interior was wood and white plaster. The wood was all varnished. The lights were just one bare bulb hanging from the ceiling.

"We can't tiptoe everywhere we go," Patrick said. "We'll never get there. Walk as carefully as you can, a real light step." He led them down the hall toward a sign at the other end. As the got closer they could read *Maternity Ward, 2nd Floor*.

"Upstairs," said Patrick pointing toward a large wooden staircase. The other three followed as he carefully climbed the stairs. At the top were two large swinging doors. Patrick pushed one door open and let Allie, Mike, and Nick go in before him. He entered last and closed the door slowly and silently.

The ward was empty, but they saw yet another sign with the word *Maternity*. An arrow told them to take a left turn about half way down the corridor. Patrick tiptoed slowly up to the corner and peeked around it. He quickly pulled back. "They're here," he whispered. The other three took turns looking. Three small men were crouched in a line outside a door under a sign that read *Nursery*.

"That's it," Mike whispered to his friends. "They're at the nursery door. I'll bet they're planning on killing Jack MacDonald in his crib. I have to hand it to Morley. This is genius. Kill him while he's still a baby. It'll be a lot easier, and there'll be a lot less questions." Allie gasped at the thought someone would kill a baby.

"We have to stop them," said Patrick. "Give me your ideas."

"They're waiting for something," Mike said, as he pondered the meaning of the scene down the corridor. "Maybe there's someone in the nursery. We need to get close enough to hear them. It would help if we knew what they were planning."

"We gotta be silent," warned Patrick. "Take every step very carefully. If they hear someone they can't see they'll know we're from the Time Institute. They might run, or they might fight."

Patrick led the way, making each step slowly and carefully. He was ready to stop in mid-step if the floor began to squeak. The others did the same. They snuck up stealthily until they were standing beside Morley and the two men. The men were fully cloaked, so the team of youths couldn't tell them apart. Patrick guessed Morley was first in line, nearest the door. He was the one who kept peeking through the nursery window.

The night vision goggles had given the four young time travelers a major advantage. They could see Morley and his minions clearly, yet the men were unaware that a Fixer team was close enough to touch them.

"The nurse is working her way down the row of cribs," the first man whispered. "I can see the babies' names on the ends. MacDonald is third on the left. When she moves far enough away, or if she leaves, we'll make our move."

Standing beside Morley, Patrick could see through the window too. He saw a woman working at a crib near the back of the nursery. He knew she was a nurse, but she wasn't dressed like any nurse he had ever seen. In his time, nurses wore scrubs. This one wore a long dress that reached almost to the floor. She had a white smock over the dress with a red cross on it. She wore a round, white cap, and her hair was tied up in a bun. Her white leather shoes looked like high top sneakers, but there were no laces. The shoes were held on her feet by rows of buttons that ran up her ankles.

The nursery was painted white. The cribs were made of bent metal and were painted white too. There was a pile of cloth diapers on a table. The bottles and jars of medicines were all glass. There was no plastic anywhere. There were no high tech machines. It all looked so old and primitive.

Morley gazed through the window again and watched the nurse as she changed a baby's diaper. "Let's go over it one more time," he said to Teller and Bryant. "Collin, cover the baby's face with this thin sheet of plastic. That will cut off its air and suffocate it. With its face covered it won't be able to cry or make any noise. Lars, hold the baby's arms and legs. Be careful that you don't make any bruises. It should be over fast.

"I'll stand guard. If the nurse hears you, and investigates I'll have to kill her with my weapon. I prefer not to. If everything goes right, Jack MacDonald will be a case of what they call crib death. It happens a lot in this time period. Healthy babies just die in their sleep. No one knows why. There won't be any investigation. There will be a quiet funeral and a small grave. However, Dr. James MacDonald will never be born.

"As soon as we are done, we get back to the craft. Chaos will start when the nurse finds the baby dead, or I shoot her. Either one will cause a change in her sequence. Chaos will spread as more and more sequences are changed: the parents, the doctors, and so on. We will be safe in the craft."

At that point the nurse left the nursery through a rear door, giving Morley his opportunity. "Let's go," the madman said to his minions. Patrick panicked. He had to do something, and he had to do it now. He pulled back his leg and drove his foot into the side of Morley's knee. Morley screamed in pain and collapsed.

Mike, Allie, and Nick saw what happened and jumped the minions from behind. Mike struggled with the one in the middle. Allie had jumped the one on the end. She wrapped her arm around his thick neck, so the man's throat was trapped in the bend of her elbow. Allie used her other hand to squeeze her arm together like a nut cracker. Meanwhile, Nick grabbed the man's arm so he could not strike at Allie. With the blood to his brain cut off by Allie's elbow, the man slipped into unconsciousness. As he passed out, he dropped to his knees, still in Allie's grip.

Mike's man fought to get free from the invisible arms around his neck, but Mike held on tight. "It's a Fixer team," yelled Morley. Mike's man became frightened and fought harder. Twelve-year old Mike was no match for a strong man, even if he was small. The minion got the upper hand. He could not see Mike, but he could feel him. He found Mike's arm and yanked the boy in front of him. Then, he spun Mike around and bent his right arm behind his back.

Morley had more trouble with Patrick. Patrick was stronger than Mike, and the professor was much older than the maintenance men. He also had an injured knee. Mike, Allie, and Nick could see Patrick and Morley fighting, while the minion holding Mike could only hear them. The minion lifted Mike's arm higher up his back so Mike cried out in pain. "Give up, or I break your friend's arm," the man warned Morley's invisible assailant. Allie and Nick saw what had happened to Mike, while Patrick only heard his yelp. The man lifted the boy's arm even higher so Mike cried louder. That was all Patrick could take. "OK. I quit," he said. "Don't hurt him."

Allie and Nick released the second man. As blood flowed back into his brain he recovered his senses. He grabbed Allie's arm and twisted it behind her back. Allie squealed in pain, like Mike had. The minion couldn't feel Nick and didn't realize there was a fourth attacker.

Morley moved behind Patrick and twisted his arm up behind his back too, so all three – Mike, Allie, and Patrick - were in the same position. "We'd better get out of here," he said to his men. "They may have sent more than one Fixer team. Meet at the craft. Take these guys with you." The six returned the way they had come in. They made more noise on the way out, but no one heard them. It was the middle of the night and the hospital was empty. The men were still unaware of Nick, who silently followed the six out of the building.

On the lawn, Morley ordered the three captives to uncloak. Patrick felt his heart squeeze in panic. If they obeyed, Morley would see the night vision goggles under his head cover and he would take them. He would have such an advantage it would be impossible to stop him. If Patrick refused to uncloak, Morley would do it for him. The adult would reach in front of him and push the switch on his chest.

With his free hand Patrick pulled his off head cover and night goggles at the same time. This way, the goggles stayed wrapped in the head cover. He put the head cover, with goggles inside, under his arm. Then, he uncloaked. Mike and Allie were watching. They saw what Patrick had done and did the same. Morley and his men uncloaked too and became visible for the first time. They pulled off their head covers to expose their faces, the same faces the boys had memorized from the photos Mr. Smith had given them. The only difference was Morley's hair color. It was now dark brown rather than white, and such a bad a dye job the three young time travelers stared at him in disbelief.

"These are just kids, Your Excellency," said Bryant. "Has the Time Institute become a kindergarten? Did they run out of adults?"

"They don't even have enough kids to make a whole Fixer team, Your Excellency" Teller laughed, looking at Allie's red uniform. "They had to throw in a Researcher. They must be getting desperate."

"How old are you?" Morley demanded, looking Patrick in the eyes and examining his face.

"I'm 12," Patrick answered. "But I'm old enough to know you guys are real jerks."

"What's your name kid?" Morley asked in the same demanding tone.

"I'm Patrick Weaver," Patrick replied again with the same defiance.

"A Fixer Team made up of two 12-year olds and a Researcher," said Morley sarcastically. "It beats me why they sent you, Weaver. I figured they would send some pros like Smith and his team.

"It doesn't matter," Morley said changing the subject. "You three had to get here in a time craft. Where is it?"

Patrick didn't answer. To loosen his tongue Teller and Bryant bent Mike and Allie over in pain. They groaned as their arms strained against their shoulders. Patrick gave up. "Besi.... It's over this way," he said pointing in the CT 9225's direction. He had almost slipped and said "Beside yours." If he had, Morley would have wanted to know how he had seen a cloaked craft.

"Take me to it," Morley commanded.

Desperate thoughts raced through Patrick's mind. He was the team leader and he was responsible for the mission. He was beaten right now, but he hoped he could change that. He still had important advantages, night vision goggles and Nick's remote, and he didn't want to give them up. If he got his team out of this mess he would need them.

As Patrick led Morley to his craft the adult added important detail. It was bad news for the boys, but it was important information. "This is good luck," Morley told Teller and Bryant. "We'll get out of here in their craft. I was afraid you two idiots had got us stuck here."

So, something was wrong with Morley's craft and he needed theirs to escape. Right now Patrick didn't see how he could stop them, but he would stay alert. He needed to act if he had the chance.

"Take off the cloak and open the door," Morley ordered the young Fixer pilot. Patrick decided to reveal a bit of his secret, but wove in a small lie. "We don't use the old cloak covers anymore," he told Morley. "Now, uncloaking and opening the door are one operation."

"Show me," said Morley. "It's about time the engineers came up with something better."

Patrick reached into his pocket with his free hand and found the cell phone. He opened it quietly so it sent a signal to the craft. Next, he pretended to cough so he had an excuse to bend over, away from Morley. While coughing, he quickly read the math problem on the phone's screen. "Thirty-three," said Patrick loudly enough for the phone to pick up his voice. The craft uncloaked and the door opened.

"Well, well," said Morley. "Isn't that handy? Did you see how that was done Collin?"

"How did you know the math question?" Teller demanded.

"You don't have to anymore. You just make up your own addition problem and answer it. That creates the brain waves," Patrick lied.

"Does it cloak the same way?" Teller demanded again.

"Yup," Patrick answered as he slipped the phone back into his pocket. Mike, Allie, and the still invisible Nick knew what had happened. Patrick had just given Teller misinformation. Maybe the minion could fly the CT 9225 out of here, but he didn't have the remote. The next time he the closed door he couldn't open it again. He couldn't cloak again.

"Into the craft," Morley told his men. The two men made the Eternal Guide salute and stepped in.

Allie, Mike, and Patrick looked at each quizzically, asking with their eyes, "What was that gesture about?" Bryant disappeared from view when he sat on one of the benches. Teller waited at the pilot's controls. Mr. Smith was correct when he guessed that Teller was the pilot and Bryant the engineer. However, on this crew Morley the S/O, was the guy in charge.

"Well, I hope you kids like 1901," said Morley sarcastically. "You're going to be here a long time. So, have fun."

"You won't get away with this," yelled Patrick.

"You sound like a character in a bad movie," laughed Morley. "You won't get away with this," he repeated in a high voice, mocking the twelve-year old pilot. "Guess what, kid? We got away. Get used to it."

Mike realized any information could be useful and decided to keep the madman talking as long as possible. "So, you plan to take over the world?" he asked. "No other dictator ever managed that. You'll have to be a lot smarter than they were, and I don't think you are."

Morley bit at Mike's bait. "Other dictators failed because they were mortal men," he hissed. "No matter how important they made themselves, everyone knew they were only men. Some day they would die, just like everyone else. Morleyism is far more permanent. I will convince the world that I am god, that I am their Eternal Guide."

"That's a pretty tall order, being god" Allie teased. She understood Mike wanted to keep the man talking. "You'll never pull that off."

"Oh, yes I will," Morley boasted. "When I kill Dr. MacDonald I will set off a wave of Chaos that will sweep through history from his time to mine. There will be nothing but war and famine. Knowledge and technology will disappear. It will be a new dark age and the world will become desperate. It will be full of miserable sheep begging for someone to lead them, to bring them order and peace.

"I will use our technology to perform miracles. I will cloak and uncloak so people see me appear and disappear. With your time craft, I will be here, and then suddenly I will be somewhere else. I will take over the world long before my own sequence. Thanks to the experience of time, I will not age. Generations of my subjects will live, grow old, and die, but their Eternal Guide will not. They will think I am immortal. They will believe I am god.

"Everyone will welcome me. If they do not, I will threaten to kill their bodies and destroy their souls. They will have no hope of a better life after death. I will hold the entire world in my hands. I will be the last and greatest dictator in history. I will be an immortal emperor-god, the Eternal Guide, Morley the Great."

Mike thought to himself, "Talk about bad movies. This guy is the stereotype of a Hollywood mad scientist. All he needs is an evil cackle."

Morley stepped into the craft. He stood in the door beside Teller and turned to face the young time travelers. "If you manage to get out of this time, be sure to visit the future," he told the three youths with a boastful laugh. "Come and witness the reign of Morley the Great, the Eternal Guide. It will be glorious.

"Now, Collin," he said to his pilot. "Go right for the target. There may be other Fixer teams on our trail, better ones than these three incompetents. Clever plans are too risky. We kill MacDonald, and then we build my empire."

Teller looked at the math problem on the craft's small screen and answered, "Seventy-six." Nothing happened. "Seventy-six," repeated Teller. Still nothing. "Seventy-six," he yelled.

"You moron," Morley howled at Teller. "Lars can't fix a time craft and you can't fly one. Do better in my government, or I'll have you both executed!"

Patrick knew it was too dangerous to keep Morley trapped in 1901. It was safer to let him go. He made up a math problem with seventy-six as the answer. "Thirty plus forty-six," he thought to himself, creating the brain wave pattern. Then, he yelled, "Seventy-six." It worked. The CT 9225 received its pilot's brain waves and the door closed.

Just as Patrick yelled his answer, a fist-sized rock appeared flying through the air. The stone made a loud "bonk" as it hit Teller on the head. As the door closed, the boys saw Teller stagger. A moment later the craft disappeared.

Nick uncloaked himself. "That was my souvenir," he shouted. "That was my Mars rock. You get it back to me."

"Nick. Nick, calm down," said Patrick. "I didn't know you took a rock from Mars."

"I wanted a souvenir," said Nick angrily. Mike and Allie knew Nick was really upset at having lost the CT 9225, not the rock. The craft was like his child and he was almost in tears.

"Well, it's Teller's souvenir now," said Mike, trying to comfort Nick with a joke. "It's a souvenir of how he got that big bump on his head. Don't worry Nick; we'll get your rock back. We'll get our craft back too."

The other three all looked to Patrick. Patrick's face fell. He dreaded having all the responsibility on his shoulders. He paused to think about a new plan.

"Well, Mike, we're stuck here," Allie said in a loud stage voice so Nick could easily hear her. "We're stuck here unless we can find someone who knows how to repair a time craft. Mike, do you happen know anyone who can do that?"

"I think I do," Mike answered as he placed his arm around Nick's shoulder. "Nick, we need you to fix their craft," he said soothingly. "If you do, we're back in business." Nick nodded but didn't respond. He just helped Mike take off the craft's cloak cover. Meanwhile, Patrick opened the door by answering an addition problem. Nick stepped in and got out the craft's tool kit. He came back out to find what was wrong.

Meanwhile, Mike, Allie, and Patrick talked about the mess they were in. "Things really aren't all that bad," Mike told Patrick. "They're stronger than we are. They overpowered us, but we're better off than before. Think about it. We stopped Morley from killing Jack MacDonald. His sequence is unchanged. Dr. MacDonald will be born and make his discovery."

"Morley and his minions still don't know about the night vision goggles," Allie added. "We can see them and they don't know it."

"We know where they're going," Mike continued. "They're headed for the Hampton Summit."

"We know Morley's megalomania has turned him into a crazy hothead," Allie said. "Get him mad and he doesn't think. He's real impressed with himself. It's easy to get him talking, and then he talks too much. We can use that to our advantage."

"We know that Teller and Bryant really stink as a pilot and an engineer," Mike noted. "They're trying to fly the CT 9225. It belongs to you and Nick, and doesn't work well for them. That's a real handicap for Morley."

"We can outsmart them," Allie continued. "They're not innovative. We are. They don't take risks. We do. We're audacious."

"To top it off," Mike added, "they just left in a craft they can use only once. You still have Nick's remote."

"When they get out of the CT 9225, they can't get back in," Allie explained. "Also, they can't cloak it. That will be a real problem for them. Where will they hide it?"

"If Nick can fix the problem with this craft, we're holding all the cards," Mike concluded. "It's Morley that's stranded, not us. Our biggest problem is he's stranded at the Hampton Summit. He's too close to Dr. MacDonald to suit me. We need to get there and make sure he doesn't carry out his plan".

"By the way, what did you think of that hair?" Allie asked Mike and Patrick with a laugh.

"What a horrible dye job," Mike responded with a smile.

"Doesn't he ever look in a mirror?" Allie wondered.

"He must have used shoe polish on his hair," Patrick added.

"He's the only guy in the world who gets a shoeshine on his head," Mike joked.

"And who calls himself the Eternal Guide?" Patrick asked sarcastically.

"Or calls someone else, Your Excellency?" Allie answered. "And what was that thing about touching their hands over their heads?"

Nick came around the craft. His sleeves were rolled up and he had a tool in his hand. "Bad news," he said shaking his head. "It's the gravity polarizer. I don't know what that pilot did, but he really messed it up."

"Didn't you fix the gravity polarizer for your Engineer second class field trial?" Allie asked.

"Yeah," Nick answered, combining disappointment with his normal worried expression. "But, this one's completely fried. I can't fix it. This craft isn't going to move again until the unit's replaced. Without a new polarizer we're stuck here."

The four time travelers stared at the ground as the enormity of their problem sunk in. They were stranded without help or hope. They had changed Mrs. Alvarez's plan, so the Institute did not know where, or when they were. It could not send help. If Dr. Morley succeeded in assassinating Dr. MacDonald and in changing history, there would never be a Time Institute to come looking for them. They would live through the rest of 20th century without aging. Through the 21st century Patrick, Nick, and Mike would grow old and die, leaving Allie by herself until she reached her own sequence. All that time, she would be alone, living in Dr. Morley's violent, bloody empire.

The four were shocked out of their gloomy thoughts when a time craft appeared. The door slid silently open and out stepped Jen Cann. "Am I ever glad to see you four," Jen said excitedly. "Finding you here was a real shot in the dark."

"You're glad to see us?" Patrick responded. "You don't know how good it is to see you!"

"How did you find us?" Allie asked her roommate. "Did the Institute send you?"

"No. They have no idea where I am," Jen answered with enthusiasm. "I watched you jump into Patrick's craft just before it disappeared. All the adults were stunned and flabbergasted." Jen was speaking rapidly and the others were having trouble understanding her New Zealand accent.

"Slow down, Jen," Allie told her roommate. "We can't follow you."

"Sorry," Jen replied, taking a deep breath to relax. "The adults - they were frozen, staring at the spot where your craft had been. I snuck into the next craft in line and took off. I remembered Nick's conversation with us about innovation and risk. I knew you had just taken a huge risk, Allie. I had to support you. I needed to help too, but I couldn't if I wasn't innovative, and just as willing to take a risk.

"Patrick, do you remember one night in the common room you dropped a bunch of papers? I bent over and picked them up for you. Pictures of Dr. MacDonald and Dr. Morley slipped out of an envelope. I didn't say anything. I just gave the papers back to you. But, I guessed those two men had something to do with your mission." Patrick shook his head. He didn't remember. The incident hadn't been important to him.

"I heard Mr. Smith say your craft only had a factory charge, so I knew you needed to go to the power plant," Jen continued. "I only had a factory charge too. So, I went there right away. I talked to the workers and they told me you were headed to Gloucester in 1901. I checked the directory. There was only one entry for Gloucester that year - Dr. MacDonald's grandfather's birth at this hospital. I guessed this is where you were. It worked. I'm so excited. Being innovative worked. I took a chance and it worked." Allie threw her arms around her roommate. The boys joined in a group hug.

"Jen," Nick said. "I need you to take me back to the hanger. I've got to get a new gravity polarizer. Morley's got our craft and stranded us here. On the way, I'll explain everything that's happened." Jen looked at Allie who nodded her agreement with Nick's plan.

"If we return to my frame of origination, we walk right into Dr. Newcomb's waiting arms," Jen explained. "I'll choose a frame at night a couple of days earlier."

Nick stepped into Jen's stolen craft. It disappeared and reappeared without moving. Nick stepped out carrying a box. Without saying a word, he walked behind Morley's craft. When he reappeared, he was done. As he cleaned up his tools he said, "Hey Allie, you really squeezed that guy's neck. I thought you were going to kill him."

"I think that's what I meant to do," Allie replied, a little embarrassed. "In my time we're proud of being non-violent pacifists. I don't know what happened to me. I just snapped when I listened to Dr. Morley talk about killing that baby. He was so cold-blooded, just like his plan to assassinate Dr. MacDonald and wipe out all our futures. I really think I meant to kill the man. I'm ashamed of myself." Mike smiled. He put his arm around her shoulder and gave her a reassuring hug that told her he was proud of her. "You know what they say about redheads," he joked to his friends. "Don't mess with them. They have fiery tempers."

"Allie, you should go with Jen," Patrick advised. "Jen, we're headed for the Hampton Summit. Wear your head covers so we can talk ship-to-ship. I plan to land on the hotel roof and find a way down

into the building. Meet us there and follow my lead.
Allie got into Jen's craft while the boys piled into
Morley's stolen craft and took their positions. "The
Hampton Summit," Patrick said to his friends. "No
need to find that sequence and frame. Pilots learn it by
heart at the Institute. Jen knows it too." He
programmed the craft, and the two strange objects on
the Addison-Gilbert Hospital lawn disappeared.

Chapter 24
The Hat Trick

Patrick slowly circled the stolen time craft over the Oakwood Hotel. He instructed Mike and Nick to don their head covers and night vision goggles so as to be ready for anything. When Patrick looked down at the roof he became angry, so angry he banged his head on the craft's wall. "Look," he said to the other two, pointing out the window. They had the same reaction. Morley had already landed the CT 9225 on the roof. The men had gotten out, but the craft only worked with Nick's remote. That meant they couldn't cloak it. So, they just left it there, fully visible, with the door closed.

Jen didn't have night vision, so all she could see was the empty time craft. Allie described to her what was happening below. The three assassins were running across the roof towards a door that led down into the building. They were cloaked and were invisible to the sharpshooters. Morley was limping and swinging his fists wildly and angrily. He was trying to find one of his invisible men to punch. Allie figured he was angry with Teller because the man couldn't cloak the craft when it landed. Patrick had fooled Teller, but Morley blamed him anyway.

It was easy to pick out Teller. He was the one with his hand on his head. He was rubbing the bump where Nick's rock had hit him. The younger and stronger Teller was far ahead of his limping leader. That's why Morley could not find him with his fist.

The time crews watched as the group opened the door to the roof and descended into the hotel. They knew they had to act fast as Morley and his team were getting dangerously close to Dr. MacDonald.

The three killers were just one of the problems facing the two crews. There was another, and it had to be taken care of first. Police and FBI snipers stationed on the roof had just seen a strange object appear. Next, they saw a door on the object open and close. They did not see the cloaked men get out. Still, they figured this was some sort of craft. They were on high alert and carefully approaching it from all directions, rifles pointed.

The marksmen encircled the CT 9225, their attention focused on it. They had abandoned their positions, leaving most of the roof unguarded. That was a bit of luck. "I think I can set down behind that big metal box on the roof," Patrick said to both his crew and to Jen in the other craft. "It will be between us and the police. We should be able to land and get the cloak covers on without being seen. But we'll have to be fast."

"HVAC," said Nick.

"What?" Patrick asked, irritated at the interruption.

"HVAC," Nick repeated. "Heating, ventilation, and air conditioning. It's not a big metal box. It's the HVAC unit."

Patrick shook his head in annoyance. "Let me see," Mike said jokingly. "Your grandpa taught you that."

"No," Nick answered seriously. "Some things I just know by myself."

Patrick landed the craft beside the HVAC, on the side away from the snipers. Jen landed beside him. "Cloaks on," he said. The five time travelers, Patrick, the two with him, and the two in the other craft, tapped the switches on their chests. Patrick and Jen opened the doors. "Quick," Patrick told everyone. "Out, and pull on the cloak covers as fast as you can." Mike and Nick, and Jen and Allie worked quickly and the two craft disappeared. The marksmen were still standing in a circle around the CT 9225 and never saw the second and third craft arrive.

"Wait here," Patrick told Jen and Allie. "I'm going to get my craft back." The cloaked Fixer team walked silently through the group of nervous sharpshooters. Patrick whispered to Nick and Mike, "On my mark." He withdrew the remote from his pocket and sent a signal to the craft. The math question appeared on his screen.

Patrick whispered "Now! Go!" His command set the others running at the craft with Patrick following right behind them. While he was running, Patrick spoke the answer to the math question into the cell phone. "Twenty three." The strange craft's door opened again, causing the snipers to back up in fear. This was the crew's window of opportunity. They leaped into the craft. Patrick immediately closed the door and the cloak came on. The startled marksmen watched the door close and the object disappear.

In an instant, the craft was far away. "Well done, guys," Patrick said to his crew. Nick and Mike knew the pilot had just saved their craft and their mission. They were proud of their leader, even though he was praising them.

"Have we changed time?" Nick asked Mike. "Do we need to worry about sequences or frames?"

"I don't think so," Mike answered. "A group of police and FBI agents on a hotel roof saw something strange. They're probably scratching their heads, but it shouldn't change their lives. I'll bet they're happy the thing went away. They won't tell anyone. I bet they won't even talk to each about it. They think they're seeing things, hallucinations, caused by stress."

"I'm taking us back to that roof," Patrick declared. Jen and Allie heard him too through their head covers. "I'll set us down fully cloaked on the sniper side of the HVAC with the door facing it. We can open the door and jump out without anyone seeing us. We'll get right back on Morley's trail. Get ready guys. Goggles and cloaks on."

The HVAC now had Morley's and Jen's craft on one side under cloak covers, and the CT 9225 on the other side. No one on the roof saw anything. No one saw the door that led down to the hotel open just wide enough for someone to slip in, and then close. If any of the snipers had seen the door move, he would have looked away rather than investigate. The police had had enough for one day. They did not want any more mysteries. They all scanned the streets below. If anything popped up, they wanted it to be a good, old fashioned terrorist, not another UFO.

On the stairs down into the hotel Patrick stopped. "When we find Morley and his men, we have to be smarter than last time. They're too strong to take on all at once. We have to split them up and beat them one at a time. Watch for opportunities."

When the group reached the ground floor they were in the back of the building. The ballroom was in front. Patrick led the crews down the main corridor toward the street and the Hampton Summit. On the way, they passed the kitchen. It had a pair of swinging doors like those in the Addison-Gilbert hospital. There were no handles because the doors push open from both sides. The doors have windows in them so the wait staff can look through. This prevents accidents.

Patrick peered through a window, examining the kitchen. It was empty. The Hampton Summit was so historic all the hotel workers had gone to the ballroom to watch. "This would be a good place," Patrick said. "It's out of the way. If we could get Morley or one of his men in here, no one could see what was happening. I don't think anyone could hear either. Let's keep it in mind."

The five invisible youths continued to move down the corridor. The floor was concrete. This time there was no worry about any squeaking floor boards, and they could move faster. They turned a corner, and again Patrick stopped. Ahead was Morley with his two men. They were lined up against the corridor wall outside the ballroom, the same way they were lined up in the hospital. The staff hadn't closed the doors yet, so Morley had a clear view into the ballroom. Jen didn't have night vision and couldn't see Morley. The boys and Allie were wearing their goggles and watched him intently. They figured he was waiting for a chance to sneak in.

Once again, Morley and his crew thought they were alone in the corridor. They had no idea the Fixer team was back, with Jen as reinforcement. Morley was fixated with what he saw through the open door. He stared in the same unblinking way a lion on the hunt stares at a zebra. The group knew he had spotted Dr. MacDonald and was imagining his mad dream come true.

Morley whispered last minute reminders to his two minions. "We're cloaked, so no one can see us. We slip in and fan out. I'll take the center. Lars, you're on the right. Collin, take the left. We'll quietly work our way across the ballroom until we're standing right in front of MacDonald. Remember how we practiced with these weapons. We'll be so close nothing can go wrong.

"I'll shoot first. I want the privilege of killing MacDonald. Then, empty your weapons into him so we are sure he dies. As soon as he's dead there will be pandemonium. Everyone will run for the doors. Move to a wall and press yourself flat against it. We are about to change the sequences of everyone in this room, so the Chaos will spread fast. We need to be in a safe place. When the excitement is over, head back to the craft on the roof. We'll have to figure out what's wrong with it. Then, we'll make our getaway."

"What about those marksmen up there?" Lars asked. "What if they moved they craft?"

"I'm betting they haven't done anything yet," Morley answered. "But even if they did move it, they can't take it far. We'll find it. Once MacDonald's dead, they'll be too busy to worry about the craft."

Patrick used hand signals to tell Allie and Nick to go back to the kitchen. He wanted Jen to go with them, but without night vision she couldn't see his silent instructions. Next, Patrick pointed to himself and then to Morley, and he made his fingers move like legs running. He pointed at Mike and placed his fingers to his eyes. Then he pointed at the minions. The other three didn't know what Patrick was planning, only what he wanted them to do. Nick, Allie, and Jen were to go back to the kitchen to wait while Mike kept an eye on Teller and Bryant. Nick and Allie left. Knowing Jen hadn't seen Patrick's instructions, Allie led her by the hand. Meanwhile, Mike pressed himself against the corridor wall. He didn't want to be in the way once the action started.

Patrick had remembered what Allie had said; Morley's megalomania had turned him into a hothead and he acted without thinking. He pulled off his head cover, but left his goggles on so he could still see Morley and his minions. The rest of Patrick's body remained cloaked. All that was visible was his head with strange eyewear.

"Morley the Great," he said sarcastically. "Morley the Jerk. You haven't got enough brains to take over the world." Morley snapped out of his trance-like stare and turned in rage to find Patrick's head hanging in the air a short distance away. Patrick uncloaked and put his hands to his ears like a pair of horns and wiggled them. He stuck out his tongue. "And where did you get that goofy hair?" he asked mockingly.

"Stay here," Morley ordered Teller and Bryant. "I'll take care of this child myself. How did you get here, Weaver?" he demanded.

"I'm smarter than you are," Patrick said teasingly. "I should be king of the world, not you. When I'm king, you'll scrub toilets. The Eternal Guide will be an eternal janitor."

"You little brat," Morley growled. "I'll teach you to speak to me like that." He took off after Patrick. Patrick jogged ahead of Morley, leading the man back to the kitchen. Morley was still limping, so Patrick did not move at full speed. If he got too far ahead, the injured man might change his mind and go back to the ballroom. So, Patrick stayed just beyond Morley's reach.

"That knee seems to hurt, *Your Excellency*," Patrick teased as he jogged ahead. "How did it happen? Did baby Jack MacDonald beat you up?" Morley was so angry he could not think clearly. All he wanted was to get his hands around Patrick's neck and silence him. The pursuit continued down the corridor until suddenly, Patrick turned left. He pushed his way through the kitchen doors and jogged to the far wall. There, he turned so he would be facing Morley when he too came through the doors. Patrick was still wearing his night vision goggles, so he was able to see Allie, Nick, and Jen. They were cloaked and standing beside the swinging doors.

Morley burst through the doors and stopped, facing Patrick. He had no idea three cloaked time travelers were in the kitchen too, standing behind him. The man who would be king uncloaked and pulled off his head cover. Patrick took off his goggles. The two stood facing each other in a final showdown.

Morley reached into his uniform pocket and pulled out his pistol. He pointed it at Patrick's chest. Shock and fear spread over the boy's face. "You're from the future. You don't have weapons," Patrick stammered, staring down the barrel of the gun.

"These weapons are everywhere in this time," said Morley with an evil laugh. "If you want one, you have no trouble getting it. Collin and Lars have them too. How did you think we plan to kill MacDonald?"

"You don't even know how to use weapons," Patrick argued, still stunned with surprise.

"Oh grow up, Weaver," sneered Morley. Then, he changed his tone and sarcastically mocked, "Oh, I'm sorry. I misspoke. You are never going to grow up. This is the last frame on your sequence. The experience of time won't spare you. Time travelers can be killed, as you're about to find out. You see, these things are very easy to use. First, I point the weapon at your heart, just like I am doing right now. Next, I pull this small lever. There's a loud noise and you fall dead. Pretty good for someone who doesn't know how to use a weapon, wouldn't you say?"

While Morley was speaking Nick scoured the kitchen with his eyes, searching for something to use as his own weapon. He spotted it, a worn out broom leaning in a corner. It had no bristles, just stubs held together by wire. He moved silently across the room towards it.

Patrick had taken off his goggles and could no longer see Nick, but he did see the broom move along the shelves and stop in front of a stack of tuna fish cans. Patrick watched two cans disappear into what he guessed was Nick's pocket. A third can, along with the broom then moved to the center of the room, not far behind Morley.

Patrick didn't know what Nick had in mind. He only knew Nick was ready and he had to act. Allie knew too, and realized Patrick needed a diversion. She cleared her throat. Morley fell for the trick. He turned his head to see where the noise had come from. Patrick only needed a brief distraction. He raised his arm and struck Morley's hand, pushing it aside. The force of the blow made Morley lose his grip on the gun. It clattered across the floor and under a cabinet.

Patrick held on to Morley's wrist and turned away from the man. He lifted Morley's arm, and pivoting under it, came up behind him. He now pinned Morley's arm behind his back, the same way Morley had twisted his at the hospital.

The Tai Kwon Do move had spun Morley around so he now faced Nick. The engineer uncloaked and pulled off his head gear. He wanted the clearest view possible.

It was Morley's turn to look stunned. He had been surprised by Patrick's move. He was surprised the tables had turned. He was surprised he had lost his gun. He was surprised that Nick was standing in front of him. He thought he was alone in the kitchen with Patrick.

Nick stared Morley in the eye. Nick always looked worried, but not now. He was angry and determined, and those feelings were etched clearly on his face. Nick's emotions were deep, but they were not complicated. He wasn't angry that Morley had tried to kill a baby. He wasn't angry about Morley's plans to kill a good man, a man that was about to help the world. He wasn't angry that Morley planned to destroy the lives of millions of people and enslave them. This man has stolen his craft, and he wanted to get even. For Nick, it was that simple.

The engineer dropped a tuna can to the floor. Then, he swung the broom over his shoulder like a hockey stick. The broom came down quickly and swept the tuna can into the air. The object flew straight at Morley and made a loud *thud* as it hit the madman between the eyes. Patrick let go of Morley, and his unconscious body slumped to the floor.

There was no time for congratulations. Still invisible, Mike burst through the kitchen doors yelling that Teller and Bryant were on their way. The two minions had waited for Morley. When he did not come back, they left the ballroom to find him. Along the way, they had taken off their head covers so they could see more clearly. They had uncloaked so they could see each other.

Of the eight time travelers in the hotel, Allie, Mike, and Jen were the only ones still cloaked. They were standing in the kitchen beside the swinging doors and could hear Teller and Bryant in the corridor.

To slow them down, Mike and Allie each leaned against a door. "We'll hold them as long as we can," Allie said. "Get ready."

Without their night vision goggles Nick and Patrick could no longer see Allie and Mike, but they heard them move in front of the doors. It was time again for action. They had hoped to take on Teller and Bryant one at a time. Now, it was do, or die, and that was no exaggeration. The two men were willing to smother a helpless newborn. Morley had been ready to shoot the nurse, Dr. MacDonald, and Patrick. He had said his two men were also armed. The four youths knew they were trapped in the kitchen with two killers at the door. Those two killers would not hesitate to shoot every one of them.

The two minions pushed on the doors with their hands. Mike and Allie's weight kept them from opening. Looking through the windows the men saw the unconscious Morley on the floor. They banged on the doors and tried to push them with their shoulders. When that didn't work, they backed up in the corridor, planning to slam their combined weight against one door at the same time and force it open. Mike and Allie looked through the window and figured out the plan. The minions had selected the door Mike was barring. The S/O knew he could not hold out against both of them, so he stepped out of the way. The door flew open and the surprised Teller stumbled into the kitchen. As the man passed by, Allie stretched out her leg and tripped him so that Teller fell forward onto the floor. Mike bent over, grabbed one of the man's feet, and held on so he could not get up again.

Bryant stumbled in after Teller. He tripped over his companion and fell forward too. While the man was falling, Nick reached into his pocket and pulled out a second tuna can that he again dropped in front himself. The broom went up and came sweeping down, lifting the can off the floor. The can hit Bryant a little high and to the right. As the man fell, Nick saw the bright red mark just above the man's eyebrow.

Meanwhile, Teller kicked at Mike and managed to pull his foot free. However, Mike had stopped the second minion just long enough for Nick to pull the third tuna can from his pocket. As Teller struggled to stand up Nick raised the broom over his shoulder. Down it came and launched the can. Teller would have been better off if he had held still, as that would have allowed Nick to take better aim. The can hit a bit low, catching the man on the bridge of his nose. Before he hit the ground, blood was already spurting from his nostrils.

Mike and Allie finally uncloaked, leaving only Jen still invisible. "Ouch. That's a broken nose," Mike observed laughing. "That's gonna hurt when he wakes up."

The four youths looked around the kitchen while the events sank in. "Nick," said Patrick. "You just pulled off a Hat Trick. It's a waste you're a goalie. Your coach should make you a wingman." The four had a good laugh, but it was nervous laughter. They had just been through a dangerous time and they were still pumped from fear and excitement. They took a moment to catch their breath and get their nerves under control.

"Well team, what are we gonna do with them?" asked Patrick.

"We need to tie them up before they come to," Mike advised. "They're not gonna be happy. They might want to fight again."

"Ideas?" Patrick asked.

"Duct tape," answered Nick.

"What?" the team leader responded.

"Duct tape," Nick repeated. "My grandpa says duct tape is the solution to every problem. I saw some over there on a shelf." Nick crossed the room and came back with a large roll of gray duct tape. He kneeled down next to Morley. "Give me a hand," he said to his friends.

The four taped Morley's ankles and knees together. They pulled his arms behind his back and taped his wrists. Next, they ran the tape around his chest, pinning his arms to his body. Finally, they stuck a short strip over his mouth to keep him quiet.

While the boys were binding Morley, Teller, who was lying on his back, began to stir. He had not taken a blow square in the head like the other two. The tuna can had hit him on the nose and had stunned him. So, he had not been knocked out cold. No one saw Teller's hand move stealthily towards his pocket. They were unaware as he silently withdrew his pistol. Teller raised his arm high enough to point the barrel of the gun right between Nick's shoulder blades, level with his heart. He pulled the trigger.

There was sequence of sounds that happened so fast it was hard to distinguish them. There was a loud bang, a clang, and a tink, followed by a yelp and a clunk. To better understand, let's slow everything down. At the moment Teller pulled the trigger, the invisible Jen stuck a cast iron frying pan in front of the gun barrel. The bullet struck the pan and clanged as it ricocheted away. Next, it made a tink as it passed through a window pane, leaving a small, round hole.

Jen yelped in fright at hearing a gunshot for the first time in her life. In a confined space like the kitchen even a small caliber pistol sounds like a cannon. Though startled, the pilot had the presence of mind to swing the pan around and clobber the man on the top of his head. The result was a resounding clunk.

The other four time travelers turn to see what had caused the commotion. Jen uncloaked, still holding the fry pan. Their ears ringing from the explosion, the others surveyed the scene. Nick realized how close he had come to dying and a chill passed over the others. The next three bullets in the gun were for them. "I stayed cloaked through the action," Jen explained. In her excitement she was talking rapidly. The others looked at her blankly, unable to understand her accent.

Allie placed her hand on Jens' shoulder. "Easy, girl. Slow down," the S/O said gently.

Again, Jen breathed deeply to relax and spoke more slowly and deliberately. "I figured if things went wrong, there should be one last surprise in the kitchen. I heard Morley describe how these weapons work. I guessed this solid metal pan would keep it from hurting anyone. He said the weapon made a loud noise, but I didn't count on it being that loud. You know, I'm beginning to like innovative thinking and risk taking," she added with satisfaction.

"You were the ace up our sleeves," Mike said.

"Huh?" Jen asked, not knowing that expression.

"Never mind," Patrick interjected. "You just saved us again, Jen. You're getting pretty good at this stuff. You're going to make a great team leader once the Institute gives you your own craft."

The boys frisked Bryant and found his gun. Then, they bound him with duct tape, just as they had done to Morley. Meanwhile, Allie and Jen kept an eye on Teller, frying pan ready if it was needed. When the boys were done duct taping Teller, Morley and his men were trussed up like Thanksgiving turkeys. "Ideas," said Patrick. "What next?"

"We've got to get them back to the Time Institute," said Mike. "We can't go over our weight limit. That means we can only send one guy at a time. The CT 9225 needs a pilot and an engineer, so you and Nick will have to make three trips. Allie, Jen, and I will stay here with the other two guys. They're helpless, so we shouldn't have any trouble. Just don't be gone long.

"There's a second problem," Allie added. "We have three craft on the roof. We need another pilot.

When you come back, bring Mr. Smith with you. When you take the third assassin back, Mike will return with him. Jen and I will go back in her craft"

"It's a plan," said Patrick. "How do we get these guys to the CT 9225?"

"Put on their gloves and head covers and cloak them," answered Mike. "We'll cloak too. Meanwhile, we'll store two of them in the corner. If hotel workers come into the kitchen we don't want them tripping over an invisible body. Three of us should be able to carry one of these guys to the roof. We just need to get him in the CT 9225 without the snipers knowing.

"Take Morley first," Allie advised. "Without him, Teller and Bryant won't know what to do, and they'll be a lot less trouble if they wake up."

It was a bit of a struggle, but Patrick, Mike, and Nick got Morley to the roof and put him in the CT 9225. Patrick and Nick took off for the Time Institute while Mike went back to the kitchen. Meanwhile, Allie had cleaned up the blood from Teller's nose. Jen had fetched Dr. Morley's gun from under the cabinet and had hid it in a trash bucket, along with Teller's and Bryant's weapons. They would end up a landfill with no one the wiser. Then, along with Mike, the girls sat next to the unconscious minions and waited.

Mr. Smith, Miss Watson, Dr. Newcomb, and the others were still on the arrival/departure pad, just as they had been when the CT 9225 had left. They were still stunned by watching Allie dive into the craft just as Patrick, Nick, and Mike left for their mission. The craft's door had closed and now reopened. Patrick and Nick rolled Morley out onto the ground.

The boys stepped out of their craft and described what had happened. They told Mr. Smith they needed another pilot to bring back Morley's stolen craft. Mr. Smith turned to Dr. Newcomb. "Charles, Dr. Morley's craft can only return to its frame of origination. It was stolen about eight months ago," he explained. "Will you have a pilot take a craft to that frame? I'll meet him there."

Mr. Smith stepped into the CT 9225 and waited for Patrick and Nick. Before they climbed in they gave Morley, who was now awake, his Eternal Guide salute. "Good luck, Your Excellency," Patrick teased.

The CT 9925 landed on the hotel roof. Nick, Patrick, and Mr. Smith ran to the kitchen. "Hi Guys. Time to take another," Patrick said. Mr. Smith expected Allie, but was surprised to see Jen in the kitchen. "We'll explain later," Patrick said to the older pilot. "Let's get the next minion to the craft." Mr.

Smith's added strength was needed as Bryant and Teller were stronger and heavier than Dr. Morley.

Patrick and Nick returned the first minion to the Institute while Mr. Smith waited in the kitchen with the two girls and Mike. They told him the story. Nick and Patrick returned again and the six time travelers carried the second minion to the CT 9225. The four Fixers and Jen and Allie were together on the roof and ready to go back when Mike realized they had a problem. "Morley's stolen craft has a cloak cover. So does Jen's. They'll become visible when we take the covers off. We'll be seen," he said.

"We need a diversion," Patrick replied. He told Mr. Smith and Mike, to wait near Morley's craft, and Jen and Allie to wait by the other. When they were in place, Patrick took off his head cover and ran around the roof yelling, "Hey, look at me. I ain't got no body."

This got the marksmen's attention and they left their stations pursuing the floating, talking head. Patrick sprinted to the other side of the roof, leading the marksmen away from two craft. In the middle of the chase, Patrick put his head cover back on and disappeared. "Go!" he yelled. On his command the other teams pulled off the cloak covers and jumped in. In a flash, the two stolen craft, Morley's and Jen's, were gone, along with the other four time travelers. Patrick climbed into the CT 9225 and he and Nick and the trussed up minion followed his friends. They left behind a group of jumpy and nervous marksmen.

Chapter 25
Return to Normal

The CT 9225 appeared on the arrival/departure pad. A couple of seconds later two other time craft arrived. Mr. Smith and Mike had left Dr. Morley's stolen craft at its frame of origination and had come back with the pilot Dr. Newcomb had sent. Jen and Allie were in the third craft. Patrick opened the CT 9225's door and he and Nick rolled out the second minion. Mike worked his way over to Allie and took her by the hand

Meanwhile, Mr. Smith talked quietly with Miss Watson and the other adults. It was obvious they were conferring about what to do next. When the adults were done he spoke to the boys. "You three have had quite an adventure. Just moments have passed for most of us here, but you've done a full day's work. We think you should take the rest of the day off.

"We are in no hurry to debrief you. We can do it tomorrow," Mr. Smith continued, stroking his mustache. "You need to file a report about your mission. But first, get some rest. Go back to your dorm. Your friends are still celebrating graduation and you should join them. After all, we did cut your festivities short. Now, there's nothing to keep you from a good time."

Dr. Newcomb addressed the boys next. "Agreed. It's not fair for you to miss out on the fun. Your friends know you are here for a special mission. We never told them what it was. In fact, we instructed them *not* to ask about it as we didn't want the public to panic. Now, you can enjoy credit for your success. Feel free to tell them everything. They might as well hear it from the horse's mouth, so to speak. We'll hear your story tomorrow. Congratulations, gentlemen. This was a job well done.

"Miss Tymoshenko, Miss Cann," he said turning to the girls. "Would you please be present tomorrow at the debriefing, as well?" The five noted that Dr. Newcomb was no longer smiling as he spoke to the Researcher pilot and S/O, but lost the thought when a group of people in white uniforms arrived. They were followed by another group in blue uniforms. Both groups spoke with Mr. Smith. The medical people went to Morley, Teller, and Bryant and cut the duct tape while the security people stood close by. The medical team helped the men to their feet and took them away. Security followed.

"What will happen to them?" Mike asked.

"Mr. Teller and Mr. Bryant will be tried. If found guilty, they will go to prison. When they are released, they will have to find a different line of work. We will never trust them around time craft again."

"And Morley?" asked Mike.

"I am sure you meant to say *Dr. Morley*," Dr. Newcomb corrected. "Dr. Morley is sick. If his tumor is back, it will eventually kill him. We don't know how long he has. His intentions were horrible. However, we can't blame him for a medical condition. He will be kept comfortable, but we will also keep a close eye on him. For years he was our colleague and friend. We feel badly."

Mr. Smith spoke again. "Now, go get some rest and have fun with the other graduates," he said shooing them off toward the dorm. Nick, Patrick, and Jen walked in the dorm's direction while Mike and Allie followed them, hand in hand. At the dorm, Allie and Jen went to their room and the boys to theirs. They showered, slept, and woke up feeling better.

Allie's and Jen's friends invited the girls on an outing in Durham. Allie asked the boys to come along. The Fixers were delighted to get off campus. They had spent most of the term studying and had not seen much of the city.

Jen informed her friends that the mission had been accomplished. The other girls were excited. The mission had been the term's best kept secret and they were the first to learn the details. Allie told them about tracking Morley and his minions to 1901, and then of fighting and capturing them. She praised the Fixers without mentioning her role. Mike would not let her get away with being humble. He bragged how she had choked the poor minion. He described how she had tripped Teller as he burst through the kitchen door.

He told how Jen stole a craft and saved them. He outlined the detective work that led her to Gloucester in 1901. He told them about Teller and the fry pan. The friends repeated over and over, "No," and "I don't believe it." Allie and Jen assured them it was all true. The friends were excited to be with this band of heroes. Patrick, Nick, and Mike would not admit it, but being a hero was pretty nice.

Back at the dorm, the news spread like wildfire, and that night, the five time travelers were the center of attention. Mike was the center of Allie's attention. She held his arm, beaming with pride. She knew a lot more about Mike than anyone in the dorm. In some ways, she knew more about Mike than he knew himself. After all, she had written a research paper about him. He was more than just Mike Castleton, Fixer team S/O and hero. He was also Captain Mike Castleton, the guy who started the music revolution known as Chamber Rock. In the 21st century this Mike Castleton and his two friends had been the famous band the Sirens. They had streamed across the sky of music like a new comet. Then, like a comet they had disappeared from music history. No one knew why. Mike had lived in the 21st century, a time when there was television, newspapers, magazines, and the internet. Yet, none of these sources had preserved any information about the Sirens. It was like someone removed it on purpose. That was crazy. Why would anyone do that? How would they do it?

Still, Allie had learned what she had hoped, what she had described to Mike as "gold for a music historian." She knew how these three boys had created such audacious music. Audaciousness was part of them. That audaciousness had just saved the world. Allie bubbled over with excitement and squeezed Mike's arm. She loved the special friendship she had with him. She loved being friends with Patrick and Nick.

A din of voices filled the common room as the graduates peppered the five heroes with questions. How could they get night vision goggles? Was Nick going to give his cell phone remote to the Institute? How did it feel to have a gun pointed at you? Could Nick show them his hockey swing? What was it like to tackle someone and fight hand-to-hand? What was the Hampton Summit like? Did they actually see Dr. MacDonald?

The party lasted past midnight. The boys struggled to get out of bed the next morning, but they had a debriefing at 9:00. They met Allie and Jen and the group arrived at Room 307 to find the adults waiting for them. Patrick gave the report.

The Institute people were curious about the mission. How had the boys figured out what to do? They were fascinated by the night vision goggles and Nick's remote. These were important abilities, to cloak a craft and open it at a distance. To never again use a cloak cover. To be invisible, but able to see other team members.

"Why did you toss away my plan?" asked Mrs. Alvarez. She wasn't angry, just curious.

"Mike told us it's easier to get forgiveness than permission," Patrick replied. "He said you would be happy if we were successful. If we stopped Dr. Morley, no one would scold us for breaking the rules."

"He was right," Mrs. Alvarez replied. "If you had asked permission to follow your own instincts, I would have ordered you to stick to the plan." The other adults nodded. "No one is upset with you. In fact, we are overjoyed. You succeeded beyond our dreams," Mrs. Alvarez concluded.

"Here's another appropriate quote," Dr. Newcomb added. "Success has a thousand parents, while failure is an orphan. We pat ourselves on the back for being the parents of your success. We're proud to be its parents. But we gave you a recipe for failure. Had you failed, I'm afraid that failure would have been all yours. It is unfair and I apologize. The Time Institute is stuck in its ways. We just don't know a lot about innovation and risk. Thank you for being what we are not."

Mr. Smith asked the next question. "I saw that Dr. Morley and Mr. Bryant had large red bumps on their foreheads. Mr. Teller took the worst of it. He had three bumps, one on his nose, one on the side of his head, and another on top. I noticed that Dr. Morley had an injured leg. We sent you back without weapons. I'm guessing that you innovated. Can you tell us about this?"

Patrick told them that he had studied Tai Kwon Do. He explained how his training had saved baby Jack MacDonald, how it had disarmed Dr. Morley. Mr. Smith noted that martial arts training, purely for defense, could be an important skill for time travelers.

Patrick told how Nick had slowed down Teller with a souvenir rock. Nick took the rock from his pocket and showed it to the adults. It was still in the CT 9225 when they recovered the craft. Patrick described Nick's skill with a hockey stick. He told how Nick had knocked out three men with some tuna cans and a broom. He told them how Allie had choked one minion and how Jen had stopped Teller with a frying pan.

When the debriefing was over Dr. Newcomb made a request. "Stay one more day. We will draw up our report this morning. We'll give it to the Institute's director this afternoon. Some changes will happen around here. Before you leave, you may want to learn what they are. We should have some news for you tomorrow."

Patrick nodded. The boys were in no hurry to leave. They liked being at The Institute. "Your classmates get their job assignments today and they start work tomorrow," Dr. Newcomb continued. "You'll find out how they begin their careers."

Dr. Newcomb turned to Allie and Jen, and again his perpetual smile disappeared. "Miss Tymoshenko and Miss Cann" he said in a serious tone. "Your conduct in this matter was inexcusable and cannot be ignored. Miss Tymoshenko, you jumped aboard a time craft with a full crew. Without approval, you made yourself part of a sensitive mission. Miss Cann, you commandeered a time craft without permission and without filing a flight plan. You flew the craft without an engineer.

"Both of you, your actions were inappropriate for anyone associated with the Time Institute. I'm afraid you have put us in a regrettable position. We have no choice but to terminate you both. Before the day is over please turn in your uniforms. Miss Tymoshenko, surrender your science observer certification. Miss Cann, turn in your pilot's license. Then, please make arrangements to leave for home as soon as possible."

Allie and Jen were stunned. Their faces fell and tears welled in their eyes. They hung their heads in shame. The boys' eyes opened wide with anger and shock. Allie and Jen had contributed as much to the mission's success as any of them. Why were they being punished? Why was the punishment so severe and permanent? "No!" Mike said standing up and banging his firsts on the table. "This is not fair." Patrick and Nick stood up with him and glared at the adults.

Patrick was the first to get his anger under control. "Dr. Newcomb," he said with emphasis. "You just thanked us for being daring and innovative. You acknowledged that the Institute does not have these qualities, and apologized for it. All of you just praised us for being audacious. Now, you're terminating Allie and Jen for being like us? It doesn't make any sense, and it's not fair. They should be praised and honored along with us. They have abilities that are valuable to the Institute."

Dr. Newcomb was surprised by Patrick's forcefulness. He looked to the other adults, a look that asked for their opinions. "I wasn't there during the whole mission," Mr. Smith offered. "However, judging from what I did see Miss Tymoshenko and Miss Cann were full participants. You have to admit Charles, it took nerve to do what they did. As Mr. Weaver said, we lack those qualities here. Perhaps we should embrace these girls, rather than punish them."

Dr. Newcomb looked at the other adults. Each nodded in agreement with Mr. Smith. "I am a minority of one," he said. "Miss Tymoshenko, Miss Cann I yield to my colleagues' greater wisdom. They and Mr. Weaver are right and I apologize for being hasty. You remain in good standing with the Institute. When we file our report, your roles in this matter will be fully acknowledged.

"Now, all of you, go and enjoy yourself with your classmates."

The graduates got together again that night in the common room. This time, the excitement was about their assignments. Jen had received her own craft, the one she had taken without permission, and an engineer. She would be leading research missions. Allie would be doing research for a group of UNH music scholars that was studying Big Bands during World War II. Allie's first assignment was to find out what happened to Glenn Miller. In 1944 the legendary band leader was flying to Paris to play for American soldiers. His plane never arrived. It was never found.

Mike agreed with Allie; this was a cool assignment. He wished he could go with her. He loved Big Band music and knew all Glenn Miller's hits. It would be exciting to hear the Glenn Miller Orchestra. Allie might even see famous singers like Frank Sinatra, Bing Crosby, or Judy Garland. What an awesome adventure she would have.

Patrick, Nick, and Mike were the only ones without an assignment. Tomorrow, they would be back in the sixth grade at Atlantic Academy. Everyone agreed that was a waste of talent.

The next day, the boys, along with Allie, Jen, and some other friends, walked to the arrival/departure pad. The same group of adults was waiting there again. "Good morning, gentlemen," said Dr. Newcomb. "It's nice that your friends are with you to see you off. I told you yesterday we would have news. Gentlemen, there is a lot we can learn from you. I am inviting you back for two weeks every term to teach. Mr. Weaver, we would like you to teach a class on self-defense. Mr. Pope and Mr. Castleton, we would ask you to teach classes on innovation and risk. If you accept, you will be youngest people to ever teach at the Institute."

The boys agreed without hesitation. Again, they got handshakes and hugs from their friends. Allie threw her arms around Mike's neck and kissed him square on the lips. Mike blushed, but he sure did like it.

"Now, Gentlemen," Mr. Smith concluded. "It's time for you to leave, and for your friends to report to their assignments."

Patrick looked at the craft waiting for them. It was the CT 9225. "Which one of us is going first?" he asked. He assumed Mr. Smith would return them the way he had brought them here.

"You're all going at once," Mr. Smith replied.

"Someone needs to bring the craft back," Patrick said.

"No," Mr. Smith replied. "We think you should keep the craft with you. You are a trained crew and a very good Fixer Team. We want you ready to go should we need you again."

"Well," Patrick responded with a smile, "I have heard it said there is no time like the present." He shook hands with the adults. Mike and Nick did the same. When they arrived at Miss Watson she hugged each of the boys.

"Will you stay here?" asked Mike.

"No," replied Miss Watson. "I will be in my office tomorrow morning. Mr. Smith will be in his classroom and Mrs. Alvarez will be back in the kitchen. There's a Mapper team in Hampton mapping the sequences that led up to the Hampton Summit. They're the other team you saw the woods. We'll stay to help them."

The other grads said goodbye with handshakes and hugs. Allie kissed Mike again and said, "Don't forget the locket and what it means."

"I never will," promised Mike, pressing the locket against his chest with his fingers. "It looks like I'll be back every year. You should take your vacation while I'm teaching. We can spend those weeks together."

"I like that idea," she said with a sad smile.

Patrick sent a signal to the CT 9225 with Nick's remote. He received a math problem on his screen and answered it. The door opened and the boys climbed aboard. As a precaution, Dr. Newcomb placed his hand on Allie's shoulder. With one last wave, Patrick closed the door and programmed a visit to the worm hole. "We need to stop at the power plant at the black hole," he said. "I want to go back with a full charge."

"My mother always says you should have a full tank of gas." Mike added. "In case of an emergency."

As the craft speeded back to earth, Mike made a suggestion. "You know," he said to his friends. "I would really like to witness the Hampton Summit. After all, it is the most important event in history."

"I'm with you," added Nick.

"Okay," replied Patrick. "It'll take just a second to change the program."

Once again the CT 9225 set down next to the HVAC on the hotel roof, with the door facing the unit. Once again the marksmen saw nothing. At the ballroom, Patrick peaked in the open door. A band was in the middle of a song. Dr. MacDonald was in his wheelchair, waiting to roll up the ramp and make his presentation. He looked a little nervous.

The boys slipped silently into the ballroom and pressed themselves against the wall so no one would bump into them. They stood not far from a table with three pretty young women sitting at it. The women were out of place at a summit of scholars and government officials. They were obviously with the band. They were so stunning the boys made note of them. All three were small. One was a redhead; another had dark hair, cut short. The third was an African-American with smooth, jet black hair.

Mike elbowed Nick and Patrick. "Look at the band," he said. All six members looked college age. A young man played lead guitar and sang. There were young men on bass, saxophone, keyboard, and drums. An African-American woman played trumpet. Their dress was strange for a rock band. They wore jackets and ties that looked like Atlantic Academy senior high uniforms. Mike noticed the singer was wearing a captain's hat and had a hot pink guitar strap. "That's my trademark!" he exclaimed angrily. "Couldn't the guy come up with something of his own? At least that's different," he sneered, pointing at a picture of a singing mermaid on the bass drum. "It's different, but it's stupid. And who ever saw a bass player that tall? Bass players are always short."

"He looks a lot like pictures of my father when he and my mom married." Nick noted.   "You have to hand it to them. They sure can play." Patrick and Mike nodded grudgingly. Yeah, the band was good, real good.

Mike was so annoyed that that the singer had ripped off his trademarks that he stepped away from his friends and marched across the ballroom floor until he reached the stage. There, he stood in front of the band and glared at the singer from up close, close enough to touch. What happened next shook him to the core. Mike was cloaked and was invisible to everyone, except his friends with night vision goggles. However, the singer looked the young S/O straight in the eye. Then, the man smiled knowingly and winked at him. It was like they were sharing a secret, something only the two of them knew. Mike was so unnerved he turned and walked quickly back to Patrick and Nick.

"He saw me,' Mike whispered, physically trembling.

"Impossible," Patrick said. "You're cloaked.

"I don't know how he did it," Mike insisted. "But he saw me. He looked me straight in the eye and smiled and winked. He knew I was there. He wasn't upset that I had walked up to the stage and was staring at him. It was like a secret, between just the two of us. I don't know how he did it."

The singer suddenly stopped playing his guitar to free his arms. He lifted them into the air with the index finger on each hand pointed upward. The boys knew it was a signal to the band. As the end of the song arrived the singer pointed three times fast at the trumpet player, who answered each point with a short note. At the third note, the singer jumped in the air. He bent his legs at the knees so it looked like he had jumped much higher than he actually had. As his feet hit the floor, he wailed out one long note on his guitar. He worked his fingers back and forth along the instrument's neck so it sounded like the guitar was trying to talk. He suddenly stopped. He turned toward the audience and bent at the waist, his arms dangling.

What came next was positively weird. The audience came to its feet. A round of applause, whistles, and shouts erupted from a room full of scholars and government officials. They were as excited as a crowd of young people at a rock concert.

At that moment Dr. MacDonald pushed his wheelchair's joy stick to make his way to the stage. The lead guitar player nodded to Dr. MacDonald, who smiled back. It was obvious they knew each other and were friends. The younger man stepped back to join the band, allowing the room's attention to focus on the man who had arranged the summit.

Dr. MacDonald rolled to the lectern where he turned his chair to face the audience. "Ladies and Gentlemen," he began. "I invited you here today and kept the reason secret. You put your faith in my reputation. Thank you for your trust. You will find it well placed."

Dr. MacDonald finished his speech and was ready to give his secret to the world. His weak muscles made it difficult, but he raised his arm as high as he could so everyone could see his hand. He extended his index finger as much as possible. As his finger turned down, popping noises broke out all around the ballroom. The invisible boys were as stunned as everyone else to hear what sounded like gun shots. They were more stunned as they watched Dr. MacDonald slump over the side of his chair. They heard one of his students yell, "He's been hit. He's been hit."

After a moment that seemed like an eternity, Dr. MacDonald slowly pulled himself up in his chair. The audience could see a large red mark right between his eyes. He reached up and gently rubbed the mark. It hurt.

The head waiter stood off to the right of the stage, very embarrassed. His wait staff stood around the room holding foaming champagne bottles. He had arranged a signal so the staff all opened their bottles at the same time. However, the head waiter had jumped the gun and given the signal before Dr. MacDonald finished. On cue, the wait staff released the corks. With a popping that sounded like pistol shots, the stoppers flew across the room. One of the corks had hit Dr. MacDonald right between the eyes and knocked him over in his chair. The embarrassed head waiter apologized repeatedly. The scientist smiled and raised his claw-like hand to assure the man everything was fine.

The audience realized what had happened and broke out laughing. Dr. MacDonald and his students had a good laugh along with them. "Now, before anything else happens, let's get this job done," he said. He pushed a computer key. At the speed of light, which everyone except three invisible boys standing against the wall knows is the fastest speed possible, the formula was sent. It was received by hundreds of computers, never to be a secret again.

One of the ballroom doors opened slightly. It stayed open only as long as it would take three people to slip out. Then, it quietly closed.

"We still have one more stop," Nick told Patrick and Mike. "We have to return these night vision goggles." Once again, it was night when Patrick set down outside the National Guard Armory. Nick got out and ran across the lawn. He placed the night vision goggles in front of the door so the first soldier to work would find them. He left a note thanking the National Guard for the loan.

As Patrick took off for the Atlantic Academy roof Nick said to his friends, "We need to get ourselves some night vision goggles. I don't want to borrow them again. We should all start saving to buy a pair." The other two nodded in agreement.

During the return trip Mike and Nick changed into their school uniforms. Patrick had left his uniform on the school roof. When the craft landed the three stepped out. Patrick picked up his uniform and went back into the craft to change.

"We gotta leave the craft here for now," Patrick said to Nick and Mike. "But we need to find a better place to keep it."

"How about the woods behind my house, where we saw the time teams? No one ever goes there," Mike suggested.

"Good idea," Patrick replied. "We'll move it when we can." The boys jogged across the roof, opened the trap door, and climbed down into the stairway. At the bottom, Patrick cracked the fire door and looked out. The coast was clear. They walked along the corridor and down the stairs, headed to Miss Watson's conference room where they had left their coats and backpacks.

As they entered the conference room they peaked into Miss Watson's office and were startled to see her working at her desk. "Miss Watson," stammered Patrick. "How did you...?"

"Frames, Mr. Weaver," replied Miss Watson. "Frames. You understand how they work." She looked back down at the papers in her hands.

As the three boys left the building Mike looked at the clock in the lobby. It read 3:58. "Twenty-three minutes," Mike thought to himself. "That all happened in just twenty-three minutes. Time travel does mess with your mind."

Their parents watched the three walk across the parking lot. They seemed different from the boys they had dropped off that morning. Usually, the boys slouched. They pushed and elbowed each other. They kicked pebbles. Today, they walked confidently, side-by-side. They stood straight and appeared taller.

Mike tossed his backpack into the van and then climbed into the passenger's seat. He leaned over and kissed Mrs. Castleton. Menlo was in the back seat. The dog leaned forward to kiss both Mike and his mother. As they wiped their cheeks Mrs. Castleton asked her son, "So, anything exciting happen today?"

"Nah," Mike answered. "Pretty normal, boring. What are we gonna do tonight?"

"Your father rented a classic science fiction movie. He wants us to watch it together," Mrs. Castleton answered. "You'll like it. The movie's based on a book by a famous writer named H. G. Wells. We'll make popcorn."

Great," Mike answered. "I really like classic movies. What's its name?"

"The Time Machine."